BAMBI'S
CHILDREN

Also by Felix Salten

Bambi
Renni the Rescuer
A Forest World

BAMBI'S CHILDREN

The Story of a Forest Family

FELIX SALTEN

Illustrated by RICHARD COWDREY
Translation by BARTHOLD FLES
Edited by R. SUDGEN TILLEY

Aladdin
New York London Toronto Sydney New Delhi

ALADDIN
An imprint of Simon & Schuster Children's Publishing Division
1230 Avenue of the Americas, New York, NY 10020
This Aladdin paperback edition February 2014
Text copyright © 1939 by The Bobbs-Merrill Company
Illustrations copyright © 2014 by Richard Cowdrey
All rights reserved, including the right of reproduction
in whole or in part in any form.
ALADDIN is a trademark of Simon & Schuster, Inc., and related logo
is a registered trademark of Simon & Schuster, Inc.
Also available in an Aladdin hardcover edition.
For information about special discounts for bulk purchases,
please contact Simon & Schuster Special Sales at 1-866-506-1949
or business@simonandschuster.com.
Designed by Hilary Zarycky
The text of this book was set in Yana.
Manufactured in the United States of America 0114 OFF
2 4 6 8 10 9 7 5 3 1
Library of Congress Control Number 2013951051
ISBN 978-1-4424-8746-8 (hc)
ISBN 978-1-4424-8745-1 (pbk)
ISBN 978-1-4424-8747-5 (eBook)

BAMBI'S
CHILDREN

Chapter One

THE DARKNESS TOWARD THE EAST was thinning now. Still the owl's cry drifted down the pathways of the forest, pale stars glimmered in the farthest gloom; but fox and marten paused from hunting, belly-deep in mist, and sniffed the coming dawn.

Trees, unwilling to awake, turned restless leaves; the birds that roosted in their branches opened round and sleepy eyes. A twig snapped suddenly.

"Who's that?" a startled magpie cried. "Who's that moving there?"

Her mate drew a sleepy head from under his wing.

"No one! Who could it be?" he chided her crossly. "Just worry, worry, worry, and it's hardly dawn ...!"

"We heard it, too, we did! There's surely something coming!" the tomtits in the bushes whispered fearfully.

A blackbird tried a fluty note. A jay, inquisitive and unafraid, screeched cheerfully:

"It's Faline, the roe-deer! Faline and her children!"

Crows came flapping from their nests.

"Faline!" they echoed disapprovingly. "She spoils her children. They have their own way in everything. Disgraceful !"

Faline turned her quiet brown eyes upward to the treetops.

"You see, Geno," she said, "what they think of me? Now, be a good boy and stop whining."

"But I'm tired. I want to lie down," Geno complained.

"He's not a *bit* tired!" His sister Gurri trotted close

to her mother's red-brown flanks. "It's just because I ran faster than he did when I played his stupid old game. He's an old sorehead!"

"I'm not a sorehead, and you can't run as fast as I can! You're just a girl, that's all you are ... !"

"I'd like to know what that's got to do with it!" Gurri tossed her head and a shower of dewdrops fell gleaming from a low-hanging bush.

"Children!" Faline remonstrated soothingly.

"Well, Mother, if he wasn't such a spoilsport! Boso and Lana wanted to go on playing, but he," she mimicked him disparagingly, "he was *so* tired!"

Angrily Geno drummed his small hoofs on the winding path.

"You'll see! I won't show you any more games!"

"All right, I'll make up my own!"

"*You* will!"

"All right, Boso will! He's cleverer than you are and he's nice!"

The crows flew away with great flapping of black wings.

"You see? What did we tell you!" they croaked scornfully. "Just listen to those children!"

"Nasty black things!" Geno scoffed. "If my father, Bambi, were here, he'd show you!"

"Ho, ho, ho!" chortled the crows. "Teach him manners, Faline!"

A woodpecker paused in his drumming at an old oak tree.

"That's it, Faline," he cried shrilly; "otherwise he'll have no friends when he needs them."

"The woodpecker's giving good advice," Faline told her son; but Geno interrupted her. He leaped away from the path-side, jostling his sister.

"Something's coming through the bushes!" Black nostrils trembled; ears peaked toward the sound.

Faline regarded him placidly. "It's only the polecat," she told him. "He won't hurt you. Don't be frightened."

"The polecat smells awful!" Gurri shied a little, nostrils closed.

"That's how he protects himself. It's good protection.

He doesn't have to run fast, or to watch forever, even in the most dangerous place."

"I'd rather run." Gurri trotted proudly, her slightly speckled coat shining with the dew.

Their mother snorted, unruffled.

"In the end, it's all the same. Birds fly, snails hide in shells, skunks smell peculiar, we run and hide and watch." They came to a tiny glade, ringed close about with fern and bush and thorny vine. High beech and ash, the sturdy oak and towering poplar, gave it dappled shade. Dogwood bloomed in season, elderberries shed their clustered fruit, privet made a deep green wall. "Perhaps even He has something that He fears, although," Faline sighed, settling herself comfortably on folded forelegs, "I doubt it."

Mention of Him shed gloom upon them for a while. They snuggled close, Geno and Gurri drawing warmth from their mother's body.

"Tell us a story, Mother," Geno begged.

"I thought you were sleepy," Gurri mocked.

Faline looked wistfully about. This was the place

where the children had been born. Here it was she had known the pain and Perri the squirrel had come, inquisitive and kind, to sympathize. Here their other friends had homes in bush and treetop: the magpie, jay and woodpecker, keen-eyed outposts who stood guard and warned when harm approached.

"What would you like to hear?" she asked.

"Tell us," Gurri's eyes glowed with eagerness, "tell us about Gobo."

"About Gobo? But you've heard about him so often."

"Never mind." For once Geno agreed with his sister. "It's so exciting. It makes the hair on the back of my neck stand up."

Faline moved her jaws reflectively.

"Well," she began, "as a child my brother Gobo was very delicate. He was small for his age, his legs were a little wobbly and he couldn't *stand* the winter."

"What's winter?" demanded Geno.

"Good gracious, must we go into that again!" Gurri said crossly.

"It belongs to the story," Geno rejoined with dignity.

Faline's eyes smiled.

"One day he'll know about winter and then he won't have to ask again; and you'll know about it, too, and realize how important it is.

"Winter," she said, wishing she herself knew less about it, "is the time when there isn't much to eat. Trees are bare, bushes blackly dead, and plant leaves shrivel with the cold. There is no sun, days are short and the sky is gray like the back of a fish.

"Then, one day before the wind, comes snow . . . !"

"Now he'll ask what *snow* is!" Gurri grumbled.

Geno arched his neck to look into his mother's eyes.

"Yes," he said, "what *is* snow?"

"Snow is white like daisies and it falls from the sky. But it is not soft or sweet like daisies. It is sharp, like a claw. It comes slowly at first, falling slowly as leaves fall in autumn, and then more quickly and more quickly. It doesn't stop when day goes, but it falls in the night too."

"It must get awfully thick," Geno said.

His mother sighed. "It does. You have to scrape very hard for food and it is *so* difficult to move from place to place. That's what made it bad for Gobo. He wasn't strong enough to bound high in the air as you must when you want to run in snow, and when He came . . ."

The youngsters shivered and drew closer to Faline.

"When He came and we had to run, Gobo fell into a drift and couldn't move. Your father, running past strong and fleet–he was no older than Gobo then, but already he was handsome and the muscles rippled under his skin like a fast-moving stream–stopped and begged him not to give up. But Gobo couldn't manage it and the two said goodbye, forever as they thought. Your father had already seen his mother die by the thunder-stick and many others of our friends as well: pheasants, hares, even the sly fox. . . ."

"And then . . . ?" urged Geno, tense with terror.

"Then one day, when we'd given up all hope, Gobo came back, plump, handsome, healthier than he'd ever been before. Mother was beside herself with joy, as indeed we all were, all, that is, except the leader. He shook his head, pulling a long face, when Gobo told how He had dragged him from the drift and cared for him.

"He wants you to grow and have antlers" he said, "and then, in the end, the thunder-stick!"

"It made us very unhappy to listen to him, but he was wiser than all of us."

"The wisest is always the leader," Gurri began proudly; but she was interrupted by a sudden bang.

Faline started. The young ones sprang quivering to their feet.

"The thunder-stick!" Geno whispered, pricking his ears toward the sound. "Perhaps—perhaps it's Father!"

Gurri began to whimper, but Faline said to them assuringly:

"There's nothing to worry about, my dears. Your father's the leader now and far too clever for any Him to get him."

She stopped as Perri came leaping through the branches, her button eyes agleam.

"They got him—that bloodthirsty marten!" she chattered gleefully. "Knocked him right out of a tree!"

Faline said comfortably: "There you are, children! Now, settle down. We must get some sleep."

The gold of the sun lay caught in netted branches of the trees; full-voiced the blackbird sang; pigeons crooned their love-songs; the cuckoo called from far and near; and like a shining dart the oriole flung himself from tree to tree, crying in his joy: "I'm so happy! So happy!"

Mice, scuttling in the undergrowth, peeped out to see how peacefully Faline and her children slept. The forest was awake. Only the hunted were asleep.

Chapter Two

AY GREW AND BLOOMED IN the forest. In a great, radiant arc the sun swung overhead, coming from the east, hurrying smoothly toward its setting in the west. Trees spread their leaves to it, the scent of grateful flowers was sweet, bees hummed, the caterpillar crept upon the frond of fern; only Faline and her children did not move until evening grayly spread across the land. Then easily they woke and slowly, with much scouting and care, returned to their meadow.

Gurri was impatient, would have hurried on ahead, but Faline sternly called her back.

"How many times have I told you!" Faline scolded. "Sometimes I think the crows are right and I'm too easy on you children! Now, stay behind me with your brother and wait until I give you permission to go ahead."

"I'm hungry," Gurri said stubbornly.

"You forget everything then," Geno gibed at her.

"That's enough, Geno!" Faline snapped. "*Both* of you remember that food tastes better when it's eaten in security."

Rather pleased with the wisdom of this observation which, she thought, even Bambi would have approved, Faline turned the last corner in the path before it opened into the meadow.

She paused there, sampling the air with sensitive nose. Shoulder-high in fern, shielded by the undergrowth, she searched every nook and cranny with sharpened eyes.

A magpie flying overhead called cheerily, "There's nothing there."

"Nothing anywhere," repeated Perri, scurrying down from the topmost branches of a mighty elm. "I assure you, I've looked the prospect over with the utmost care, and there's not the slightest danger anywhere."

She sat upright on a sturdy branch, her tail spread above her, her hands folded on her spotless chest.

"Are Aunt Rolla and Boso and Lana there yet?" Gurri whispered impatiently.

"No," answered Faline.

A rushing flight of duck swept overhead; a heron, his long, thin legs held stiffly out behind him, went like a ghost through the darkening sky.

"They would be late!" Gurri said.

Perri said again, twitching her nose at them: "I tell you, everything's all right. You can't see half so far as I can."

Step by step, braced for a sideward jump and quick retreat, Faline emerged into the open grass. From an elder thicket came the mellow song of the nightingale.

"You can come now," Faline called softly.

The young ones bounded out, nuzzling their mother, seeking the soft grass.

"There's Boso," Gurri cried. "Look! Aunt Rolla, Lana and Boso!"

The three came wandering across the field, Rolla sedately feeding while the youngsters played together and, now and then, nibbled a little themselves. Gurri hurried toward them with charming awkwardness, Geno following more slowly with timid leaps, frequent hesitations and impetuous, knowing tosses of the head. Boso and Lana came to meet them in such a rush that they had to spread all four legs wide to stop.

Boso began to talk at once. "There's a most extraordinary creature over there," he said breathlessly. "I don't know what it is...."

"Over where?" Gurri asked.

Lana tossed her head. "We'll show you. Come on."

Geno objected rather loftily. "Do you suppose whatever it is is just sitting there waiting for us to go and see it?"

"Oh, it can't walk fast. Perhaps it can't walk at all. What do you think, Boso?"

"I don't know. I never saw anything like it before.

I thought perhaps *they'd* know, but, of course, if Geno's not interested . . ." Boso fell to cropping the grass as though he had dismissed the whole matter from his mind.

Geno said, "Well, I suppose it's just a snail, but if you want me to go . . ."

"Come on then!" Lana urged.

Boso sprang away, Gurri and Lana at his heels, Geno lingering in the rear.

"Come over here!" Boso called.

Gurri was already peering at something half-hidden in the shadow of a clump of sedge grass.

"It's a very *peculiar* thing," she said, "but I don't think it's dangerous."

Geno trotted over, impelled by a curiosity he could not restrain. The thing on the ground stared at him with sullen, beady eyes. Geno felt a shudder run along his spine, but he made up his mind to sniff this thing. He did so, and sprang back, his four legs stiffened with dismay.

"He pricks!" he cried, rubbing his nose in the cool grass.

Gurri and Lana felt impelled to try it too. Warily they sniffed at the stranger and jumped delightedly into the air.

"So he does!" they cried.

"Hey, you!" Boso said to him. "It's wonderful to have things like that all over you, but you needn't prick us. We won't hurt you."

"Oh, no," Geno assured him, "we wouldn't hurt anything!"

The hedgehog raised his prickles in a fury.

"You'd better not try," he said grimly.

"How marvelous if we had spikes like that," sighed Lana, "long and sharp and pointed!"

"Lots of things would be easier," Gurri said, looking sideways at Boso.

"There's no call to be making fun of me," the hedgehog said surlily.

"Oh, but we're not!" Gurri cried. "Really we're not!"

"Who are you, anyway?" Boso asked.

"None of your business," the hedgehog growled.

"Say, you're pretty rude, aren't you!" Geno expostulated.

"I know how to keep myself to myself."

"So does the polecat," Gurri murmured.

"Polecat! Huh! Fine goings on, I must say!" The hedge-hog erected his quills even higher than before. "I'd be obliged if you'd let me pass," he said haughtily: "otherwise I cannot be responsible for the consequences!"

Geno glanced at Boso. "Maybe we'd better let him go."

"I think so," Boso agreed. "He really *is* very unpleasant."

The four of them started to canter away, but Gurri turned back.

"Please forgive me," she asked. "I didn't mean to be rude."

The hedgehog raised his fine black nose. "Huh!" he sniffed and waddled disdainfully away.

Gurri watched him go before turning to run after the others. Boso was galloping at full speed in a circle.

"Boso's the fastest!" Lana cried.

Gurri increased her own speed.

"Danger, danger!" she called to them.

Immediately Geno broke into wild flight. Gurri

stopped the others trying to catch up with him, and shouted:

"It's all right, Geno, I was only joking!"

He was quite breathless when he understood what she was saying and stopped to wait for them to rejoin him.

"That's no joke," he said bitterly, trying not to let his heaving flanks reveal how hard he had run. "Why did you do it?"

"Because I wanted to show that you are the fastest," Gurri explained.

"He is, too," admitted Lana.

"If I hadn't known it was a joke, *I* should have run faster," Boso argued.

"I wonder what our mothers are talking about," Gurri interposed.

"They certainly have their heads close together!" Boso looked about him eagerly. "What are those things sparkling in the trees?"

"Oh, but they're pretty," Lana exclaimed. "Let's find out what they are!"

Faline and Rolla were talking together as they grazed. Rolla was worried.

"Really," she sighed, "I declare I don't know what to do!"

"What do you mean?"

"Well, the time is coming for the Princes to be seeking us. . . ." Rolla hesitated.

"Well?" prompted Faline.

"Well . . ." repeated Rolla. She pretended there was something up-wind that engaged her attention. She sighed again. "I'm wondering—whether I shall join up with one of them again."

Faline's dark eyes glowed with restrained amusement. "I expect you will," she said comfortably.

Rolla bridled. "It's all very well for you," she said with a show of irritation. "You're happy; you have Bambi!"

"Yes," Faline smiled, "you're right; I have Bambi."

"He doesn't come to see you very often!" Rolla was annoyed with herself for the faint pang of jealousy that disturbed her; but Faline was not distressed.

"He has great responsibilities as a leader," she said quietly. "I must make sacrifices."

Rolla was suddenly ashamed. "Yes, yes, of course!" she said. "To be the leader is not all fun and clover, and to be the leader's mate must be even more difficult at times. I'm glad I'm not ambitious."

"I'm not either," declared Faline. "Believe me, I sometimes wish he was just a member of the herd."

"You don't at all," Rolla mocked her, "you know you just burst with importance!" And then, with an access of seriousness, she added: "But doesn't he ever come to see the children?"

"Not often," Faline admitted, "and then it's during the day when they're asleep and he has no duties."

"You mean, they've never seen him?" Rolla was quite horrified.

"Never. But somehow we feel that he is near—that he is thinking of us and watching over us."

"But don't you ever call him?"

"Never. I'm not allowed to, you know."

"Poor Faline!" Rolla said softly.

They grazed for a while before they spoke again; then Rolla said, as though she had reached a final, unchangeable decision:

"I shan't call anyone, either."

It was now full dark. The cry of the owl haunted the night: "Haah-ah, hahaha, haah-ah!"

Bats zigzagged in ghostly flight, darker than darkness, quieter than primeval quiet.

At the forest's edge appeared a sturdy roebuck. He grazed eagerly, raising his antlered head the while to gaze about him. Gurri came running timidly to Faline.

"Is that Father?" she asked.

"No," Faline told her, "that's just one of the young bucks."

"He's handsome!" Gurri said.

Geno said to Boso: "Is the Prince over there your father?"

Sadly Boso replied: "We have no father, now. He died by the thunder-stick."

"We never saw him," Lana added. "It happened before

we were born. But mother tells us lots about him."

"My father's the leader," Geno said proudly.

Gurri came trotting back. "He's just a young buck," she announced disdainfully, "no one for us to think about."

"What about the sparkly things?" Boso asked.

"I forgot to mention them!" Gurri stamped her fore-foot in the grass. "Let's go back."

They hurried to the spot where Faline and Rolla had resumed their grazing.

"What are those pretty little sparkly things?" Lana cried.

Faline said, "They're little stars that disobey their parents."

"Oh, I don't believe it!" Gurri said.

Faline shook her head. "Yes, they are. You see, when you're young and foolish it doesn't matter where you may be, you always think that you'll be happier some-where else. And so the little stars you see twinkling in the sky keep thinking: "Oh, how happy it must be down there on earth!"

"Of course, the big stars know better, because they've had a long time to see what goes on down here: how it's so hot in summer that the green grass dries up for want of rain, and how in winter the streams freeze over and the snow comes down to cover everything."

Geno started to say, "What's snow?" but he caught his sister's eye upon him and thought better of it.

Faline went on: "All the little stars are very happy at first, but some of them become inquisitive until they can't *bear* not to know what's going on down here, and so they fly down. And that's a very dangerous thing to do."

"Why is it dangerous?" Geno asked quickly.

"Some day, my son, you'll fall into a pit, and then you'll find out how much easier it is to go down than it is to come up again."

"What's a 'pit'?"

"Oh, Geno!" Gurri cried angrily. "Please go on, Mother."

"Well," Faline said, "they fly down and down, but when they get here they are quite exhausted, and what with there being nothing to eat on the way and one thing and another, they become smaller and smaller, until finally all they can do is glitter and sparkle a very short while in the shadow of the bushes before they die."

"How sad!" Lana murmured.

"It's always so when people don't know how well off they are," Faline said wisely. "I heard an old buck tell the herd once that more of his generation died from thinking that the grass was greener in the next meadow than from any other reason."

"Do you think the stars are happier where they are up there than we are down here?" Geno asked.

"Why, of course," Faline said, "everybody knows that! There are always grass and flowing streams up there, and no fierce animals or thunder-sticks."

"It seems to me that you're as bad as the little stars, Mother," Gurri said pertly.

She danced off in chase of the fireflies, followed by the others.

"I think it's brave and splendid of them to come," she said to Boso.

Geno heard her and chimed in: "Living and keeping

safe is much more splendid." He looked very superior and wise when he spoke.

Gurri tossed her head. "You *would* say that!" she mocked him.

Rolla and Faline watched them go.

"It's wonderful to be young," Faline sighed.

Rolla said, "Oh, I don't know! There's a lot they miss!" She glanced at the young buck out of the corners of her eyes. "How did you know all about the fireflies, Faline?"

"My mother told me about them when I was little. The stories go on. Forever, I sometimes think."

"Do you know what I've noticed about them?" Rolla asked.

"What have you noticed?"

"That they come only once, at this season of the year when the grass is young and green and the cuckoo calls."

"Oh?"

"And that," Rolla said, "is also the time when the Princes come."

The smile dawned again in Faline's eyes. "But of course," she said seriously, "that doesn't interest you a bit!"

Rolla stared at her doubtfully. "You're making fun of me," she said at last. "But," her voice grew heavy, "if you'd ever seen your mate struck down by the thunder-stick, broken and bleeding . . ."

"Poor Rolla!" Faline's eyes were soft with compassion. "I'm sorry. I'm afraid I'm thoughtless. . . ."

From the end of the field Geno gave an excited call.

"Oh, look," he cried, "here's one that doesn't move!"

The rest gathered round the glowworm quiet on a sorrel leaf.

"He's resting," Gurri declared, "resting before he flies back home again."

The glowworm shimmered regularly as a pulsing heart.

"He'll never get back," Lana declared. "He's far too tired."

Gurri whispered softly to it, "You'll get back, won't you, little sky messenger! You'll get back!"

Just then the glimmering pulse-beat slowly died.

"He's gone out!" Geno cried with awe in his voice.

"Done for!" Boso said, and turned away.

All of them turned to leave except Gurri, who remained leaning close to the glowworm. As though by force of will she had pumped fresh life in it, it began hesitatingly to blink again.

"Geno!" she cried triumphantly, as the tiny torch was born again strongly. "Geno, it isn't dead! It's alive! Alive!"

The drumming of her triumphant hoofbeats rumbled on the turf.

Chapter Three

 AWN CAME AGAIN; THE TIME of play was over.

There was a hare beside the homeward path, sitting in a little open space in a thicket.

"Greetings, Friend Hare," said Faline.

The hare raised both long ears.

"Greetings, greetings!" he muttered hurriedly. "Oh, yes, of course, most certainly–greetings!"

His whiskers trembled woefully. He seemed depressed.

"Are those your children?" he asked, rolling worried eyes at them. "Fine, healthy children, Ma'am, if I may say so! Oh, yes, indeed! Quite fine! Quite healthy!"

"Do you think so?" Faline echoed, pleasure in her voice.

"Oh, yes, I think so, Ma'am! Everyone must think so." He dropped his ears when Geno looked at him. "Oh dear, my boy," he said, "you must take care! I swear you must! Beware the cruel fox!"

His voice grew quite gloomy. His whiskers drooped.

"I can run faster than the fox," Geno remarked.

"Run faster!" The hare's nose quivered with what might have been derision. "Have you ever seen *me* run? When I was younger–rasher, too, my boy–*I* ran some races! I daresay I'd have beaten you, when I was in my prime. But look you, sonny, running isn't everything. There's cunning, too, and treachery as well. Cunning and treachery!" he muttered. "Cunning and treachery!"

"I haven't seen you in the meadow lately," Faline said.

"Me, in the meadow! Ma'am, you must be joking; Ma'am, you must be! Forgive me if I do not laugh too heartily. The matter's grown too serious. Here I sit by this thicket as you see. One jump, and I vanish, oh, quicker than trout, Ma'am, I assure you. I believe, Ma'am, on my honor, the quickest thing you've ever seen."

He stiffened suddenly, rising up until his ears and body made an exclamation point. Geno jumped himself, his four legs taut.

"What is it?" he demanded nervously.

The hare's short forelegs pawed the air with fruitless fear.

"Do you hear anything, Ma'am?" he quavered anxiously. "Is there something moving over there?" He leaped round like a jack-in-the-box. "Or is it there?"

Faline calmly sniffed the air. "There's nothing, hare. You're much too nervous."

The hare was so shocked that he forgot to tremble.

"Ma'am, how can you? With those dear children, too!" He turned to Geno. "Son," he said, "believe me, I'm the first in admiration of your mother. I swear I am, upon my whiskers! A remarkable woman, I always say, and I don't care, within reason, who hears me say it. But

I'm getting on in years, my boy, and I say to you, oh, yes, with *emphasis* I say it: you–cannot–be–too–nervous!" He came down on four feet and wiggled his ears.

"I'm not so sure of that," said Gurri.

"Oh me! Oh my! Cunning and treachery! Cunning, my dear, and likewise treachery! You are young, of course, to know the depths of treachery and cunning to which some–who call themselves animals, mind you– can sink. Why, only yesterday . . ." He paused. His voice died.

"Yes?" Gurri prompted him.

"Only yesterday," he went on faintly, "I swear to you I wasn't a couple of jumps from the bushes. There was a dandelion, a very succulent vegetable to which I am, perhaps, too much addicted, and for once I swear I knew a little peace. Not two jumps from the bushes, mind you, as safe, I should have thought, as–as that poplar there, and then this scoundrel . . . Oh, my dear, in the blink of an eyelash, the fox jumps from the very spot from which I came. Can you imagine? I was there–I was gone," he flicked his ears, "like that! But I've had palpitations ever since, and, at my time of life, that's not so good."

"Wouldn't it be better," Faline suggested, "if you went back into the field?"

"I've asked myself the question, Ma'am, really I have. But then there are the owls, you know, and which is worse, owl or fox, I really can't decide. But this I do know," and here the hare looked at Geno with ears as straight as candles, "I've only reached my present age by cultivating a state of continuous nervous prostration. I recommend it highly. It's uncomfortable, but safe. At least I hope it is! Oh dear, indeed I do!"

Faline drew away, murmuring, "Goodbye, poor hare!" as she left and Geno and Gurri trotted close behind her. The last that Gurri saw of the hare was when he resumed his endless vigil, jerking first this way, then that, his forepaws trembling against his spotless belly.

The day wore on. The air was laden with the perfume of astringent fern, of grass that lay green in the sunlight, of flowers that bloomed along the mossy paths. Woodpeckers hammered at the bark of trees and laughed a while and used their surgeon's bills again. The ruddy vest of the robin gleamed among the foliage of trees.

Faline and her children slept in contentment, lulled by none but reassuring sounds; yet suddenly Faline was wide awake.

"Geno!" she cried. "Gurri, wake up!"

"What is it?" Geno, stricken with a pang of fear, was on his feet at once. Gurri stood beside him trembling.

"Don't stand there trembling," Faline commanded with the full voice of authority. "It is your father!"

"Father!" they cried together; but Faline said, "Quiet, children, until your father speaks to you!"

She advanced proudly to where the brush was densest.

"Greetings, Bambi!"

The answer came in a deep, calm voice:

"Greetings, Faline!"

Majestically the great buck trod the underbrush, his head gravely proud, his dark eyes luminous and serene. Crowned with his mighty antlers, many-branched

and armed with long bright points, he came into the clearing.

"Children!" he said. His might was gentled. They knew no fear of him.

"We see you, Father!" they replied.

"Are they good?" he queried of Faline. "Do they behave as they should?"

"They are good children," Faline answered. "Perhaps Geno is overnervous."

"That's well, my son. You'll live the longer. But I have heard that his politeness fails at times, Faline. Why is this?"

"I think it's nervousness again."

"I see. Then, my son, learn to be careful and cheerful at the same time. You may need friends, and courtesy is the way to make them. One day I will teach you. In the meantime pay good heed to your mother and obey her in all things."

Geno hung his head beneath this reprimand and Gurri allowed her gaze to wander to her mother. When they looked for Bambi again, he was gone.

"Father!" Gurri cried in astonishment.

Faline stood quite still, her head thrown up, her nostrils twitching.

"Your father's gone," she said at last.

"But," Geno stammered in bewilderment, "I never heard a sound!"

"Our father doesn't make a sound," Gurri responded proudly. "He's the leader."

"That's right." Faline settled herself back on her haunches. "Now for the rest of our sleep."

They all three lay down side by side; but for a while Geno did not close his eyes.

"My goodness," he was thinking, "I make more noise than that, even when I just breathe!"

A fly droned by on wings of mist. The fly made more sound than Bambi!

Chapter Four

THE HARE DISAPPEARED BEHIND A bunch of tall sedge grass as though he had been jerked there on a string. His old nose bobbing above the grass like a cork on troubled water, he drew a length of dandelion inside his working jaws.

"Oh, my soul and whiskers!" he muttered. "Oh, calamity!"

Faline and her children were watching from the edge of the wood. They had been to the pool to drink, the same pool on the far side of the meadow that had tempted the hare from his post beside the path to adventure in search of greenness.

They watched the fox, his red coat gray with dust, his long black tongue lolling from his jaws, limp toward the water.

There was no breeze. The red and acid morning stifled in a sulphur-laden calm. Even around the pool a rim of mud baked into crystal shapes.

The fox was thirsty.

Geno whispered nervously, "Let's go, Mother!"

Faline did not move. "No," she replied quietly. "The fox can't scent us, nor the hare either. I hope the silly creature realizes that."

Near a clump of rushes bordering the pool a heron stood motionless on one long, thin leg, his great bill buried in the feathers of his breast, his eyes lowered in scholastic brooding over the oily water. A brace of ducks, which had been floating aimlessly in his vicinity, scuttled for the deep cover of the rustling reeds. The heron glanced up, disturbed by their agitation.

"Oh, it's you, is it!" he said in nasal, measured tones as the fox came to the water's edge.

The fox hesitated momentarily. He had been misled before by this bird's ancient, creaking appearance and knew the power and speed of that mighty bill.

"Ah, yes!" he said as expansively as the dryness of his throat would let him. "Just passed by for an eye-opener. I'm in rather a hurry, you know."

The heron cocked a filmy eye at the copper fan of threatening light which the rising sun spread on the eastern hills.

"An eye-*closer*, I presume you mean," he said pedantically.

The fox grinned obligingly. "Ah, yes, of course! Very good, ha, ha!" He lowered his muzzle to the water's edge. "Do you mind?"

The heron carefully changed his weight from one leg to the other.

"Not in the slightest," he admitted. "Only, don't start anything around this pool. This is *my* territory. I—ah—have some standing hereabouts!"

"You certainly have," the fox agreed, eying the heron's slender, horny limb. "Though," he added to himself jeeringly, "it's difficult to believe!"

There was silence except for the steady lapping sound of the fox's tongue. The hare remained petrified in shivering stillness, his front paws close as though in prayer.

Gurri said, regarding the fox, "He's got a very pretty coat."

"And an even prettier set of teeth!" Faline admonished.

"Then, what are we waiting for?" Geno whispered.

"The hare might need some help," Faline said. "If the fox saw the hare and we made a disturbance, perhaps he would hesitate long enough to let the hare get away."

"Couldn't he catch us?" Geno asked distrustfully.

"No. We've got too good a start and he couldn't scent us on this baked ground without a breeze helping him."

"I wish a breeze would come—afterward, of course," Geno said.

"What we need," their mother told them, "is rain.

Then the grass would grow green again and the forest plants fill, grow strong, with sap." She sighed; but later she brightened up again. "At least," she said, "when it's dry, there are no midges."

"Why is that?" Geno asked.

"Because *they* die of thirst, too, stupid!" Gurri rejoined scornfully.

"You're quite wrong." Faline reached upward to what looked to be a tender leaf without letting her attention wander from the drinking fox. "It's because the midges' eggs can only hatch in wet or marshy places. When the earth is dry and dusty, the eggs dry up and wither too."

"See, smarty!" Geno gibed at Gurri.

The fox finally drew back from the cooling water, the drops shining on his whiskers and spilling over from his jaws.

"That was good!" he said, licking his nose. "Makes me feel like a new fox!"

"I'm afraid you'll never be *that*!" the heron said dryly.

The fox started to grin again in what he thought was a way to gain favor; but, remembering that his thirst was slaked and that there was no further need to placate the heron, turned truculent instead.

"Think you're funny, don't you!" he sneered. "Well, let me tell you . . ."

The heron opened an eye that had suddenly become piercing. As though it were a little thing to which he gave no thought at all, he brought down his other leg and stood upon them both.

"Tell me what?" he inquired in a voice like an engaging buzz-saw.

The fox's eyes fell. "Nothing," he mumbled. "I was about to say—er—it looks like thunder!"

"Really!" The heron took a high and dignified step forward. "I thought you were in too great a hurry to waste time talking of the weather!"

The fox turned his back, glancing suspiciously over one shoulder.

"You're quite right," he snarled, "far too busy to spend time arguing with *you*! I'll wish you good morning!"

Together, from their respective places, the heron, the hare, the two ducks, Faline, Geno and Gurri watched him trot swaggeringly away until distance made him seem quite small and insignificant.

The heron returned to calm contemplation of the water's depths; the hare scurried round the pond and back to the wood, muttering:

"Cunning and treachery! Oh, my soul and whiskers, what a terrifying experience!"

He shied when he saw the roe-deer and only hurried on the faster, his white cotton-spot of tail gleaming as he went. The two ducks lurched arrogantly back from the reeds. They re-embarked upon the water, flirting their stubby tails, dipping their bills and shaking the drops from them.

"Wa-ak, wa-ak!" they squawked derisively.

"Come," Faline said, "it's time to sleep."

Silently the deer returned to their tiny clearing, but Geno could not sleep. He felt the oppression and tension in the air and he fancied that the trees and plants spoke together.

The leaves of the trees hung supine, without life or moisture.

"Whisper, whisper!" they went dolefully; and like an echo returning through the forest glades: "Whisper, whisper!"

At last he thought he understood what it was they said with such long sighs and stealthy rustlings:

"Rain . . . please give us rain!"

He heard a dead branch fall somewhere, and the leaves seemed to shudder at the foreboding sound. Only the great poplar remained, dark and inviolable, towering undisturbed above them all.

Geno felt his own eyes growing heavy when he heard again that patient prayer:

"Rain . . . please give us rain!"

There was, Geno decided, something awesome in this patience. There was no upbraiding, no hysteria; yet it was remorseless.

The great oak said sternly, "Two hundred years have I remained in this place, following the precepts of our kind. Shelter I have given to the earth and to all living creatures. I have borne my fruit in season. My arms are strong, but only in the cause of peace. The nourishment lent me by the earth in time of growth I returned with proper interest with the fall of leaves in autumn. . . ."

"It is so," agreed the maples. "If this is evil, we should die for it."

"It is not evil," said the chestnut, calmly firm.

This, Geno realized, was where terror lay: it was the terror of the final truth. Trees were without passion, malice, fear or envy. Moveless, invincible and uncomplaining, they spent their lives in service.

In his half-dream a poison ivy spoke in purring tones. It twined about a slender sapling that had its stunted growth within the shadow of the oak.

"How can you listen to such nonsense?" it began. "You have your rights! Better that these smug trees should die; then you can grow."

The sapling shivered.

"Quiet, parasite!" interposed the sturdy beech. "We can do without agitations of your sort!"

All at once, as though in an ecstasy of excitement, the poplar high above them swayed and threshed its branches. Geno cried silently:

"What is it, poplar?"

Again he thought he heard that ghostly echo:

"Yes . . . what is it, poplar?"

But the poplar only answered incoherently. Its leaves and branches hissed with urgency above them all. It swayed and trembled high above them in the gray.

For the first time Geno noticed that the morning did not get brighter as it should. There was a darkness in the sky, a new and livid color of dark that seemed to bring the treetops closer to the ground, and that seemed to be filled with the scent of sulphur and a great humming force.

Now the other trees began to tremble in the order of their size: the tall elms first, the maples and the oaks that shivered on their sturdy trunks, and then all of them were trembling, their dry leaves shaking and sometimes falling, spiraling, to earth.

Geno was afraid. Like the trees, he shivered also. He woke Faline in fear.

"Mother!" he cried urgently. "Wake up, Mother! Something terrible is going to happen!"

Then came the rain.

It came like lances hurled by an evil host. It beat with a loud drumming in the trees. It hurled itself on the lesser plants, pressing them down. It was dark as night until the thunder came.

A bolt of lightning tore the sky. It lighted the tortured trees, it lighted the hidden avenues where nothing moved. It flashed also on Bambi, standing before them like the spirit of the storm, his great antlers proud against it, his coat aflame with fire reflected in the rain. He trumpeted, piercing the mêlée of the storm:

"Don't be afraid, nothing will hurt you! Faline, avoid the higher trees, above all the poplar. Keep among the outer bushes of the wood!"

Lightning and thunder died. Darkness returned. They could not see him, but they knew that he had gone.

Faline said, "Come! Let us hurry!"

They went without care, at a full, stretched gallop, from the swaying canopy of trees; and as they left there came a dazzling flash. They faltered, blinded, peering fearfully back.

Lightning had struck the poplar, splitting it from top to bottom. The smell of burning added the last impetus to their flight.

The wind dropped. Huddling closely in the underbrush, they watched the rain beat straight down around them, splashing and leaping in the puddles that it made.

The air became cooler; the sky less gray. The smell of sulphur went altogether from the air.

Trees seemed to sigh and stretch. The little plants revived. Fern scent refreshed the air again.

"Poor poplar!" Geno sighed.

"It's the penalty of greatness," Faline said with gravity.

The sun burst out, turning the last shower to sparkling crystal. Gurri leaped joyously into the air.

"Let's go to the meadow to dry!" she cried. "I'm cold. A run would be fun!"

"Listen!" Faline commanded gravely.

A jay screeched twice. A magpie gave a warning chatter. From somewhere in the field a crack rang out.

"The thunder-stick!" Geno quavered.

"This is the most dangerous time," Faline told them. "Your father taught me that."

Gurri gave no answer. She stood motionless, her head thrown back, her ears twitching. The jovial chorus of the birds, which momentarily had ceased, began again. From afar, but faintly audible, came a second crack.

"I'm hungry!" Gurri complained peevishly; but she had to wait.

Not until full darkness had fallen did Faline move into the open with her children.

Chapter Five

WEEKS FLEW BY: WEEKS OF FINE, warm sun and cooling showers, of happy play-nights spent in the meadow, of restful days of muscle-building sleep. The coats of Geno and Gurri lost their youthful dapple, became a deep and even red like Faline's.

Complete contentment would have been the youngsters' lot, if Geno at least had not noticed that his mother was preoccupied. Day by day she seemed to leave more to him. It was he, now, who searched the thicket; he, more and more, who scented out the field at evening and led them in.

He was aware of a double sense of pride and nervousness. He tested his muscles now, not from a sense of childish arrogance, but from a newly acquired feeling of responsibility.

When he galloped in the meadow he checked his speed, measuring himself against a flying bird. He turned rapidly, side-stepped, glided into cover.

He listened to the sound he made when he moved through brush, trying to reduce it, trying to become a shadow of flesh and blood that made no more noise than a real shadow.

And when he was not so engaged, he thought of Faline, of how absent-minded she seemed and what it boded.

He tried to discuss the matter with his sister Gurri, but she did not seem to be impressed. She changed little, he thought; gaining no sense of responsibility, becoming, if anything, more willful, less imbued with the creed of care and watchfulness.

He was thinking of this one night when he stood alone near the rushes by the pool. An old, gnarled apple-tree shaded him. He was all but invisible.

Gurri was in the open, playing with Lana; but Boso seemed to have his own solitary and anxious thoughts for he, too, was not to be seen. Faline and Rolla couched together amiably, conversing quietly, chewing absent-mindedly on mouthfuls of tender grass.

Deeply immersed in thought, Geno started with terror when a screech-owl cried immediately above him:

"Oo-y, oo-y!"

Geno glanced upward and saw the bird wheel upon stiffened, outspread wings and perch on a limb of the apple-tree.

"Hi!" said the screech-owl. "Did I frighten you?"

Geno flicked his ears impatiently. In his thoughtful mood he had no desire for banal conversation with the screech-owl.

"Ho, ho, ho!" chuckled the bird. "I did, didn't I?"

"Not in the least!" lied Geno. He bent his head and nibbled at the sward. "I should think," he went on distantly, "that you'd be too old to amuse yourself with such nonsense."

The screech-owl blew out his feathers irritably. "Let me tell you," he snapped, "that everything is relative. You may be old at the age of two. As for me, I live longer."

"What do you mean, 'Everything is relative'?" Geno became very sarcastic. "Do you mean you're an aunt of mine or something?"

"I mean . . ." The screech-owl shuffled along the branch until his outline disappeared in shadow and all that was left in Geno's sight was a pair of steady, blazing eyes. "How could I be your aunt?" he demanded indignantly. "I never laid an egg in my life, and don't expect to. Much speech makes little sense, if you ask me, and—er—er—"

"It seems to me," mocked Geno, "that to sit around and say nothing is an easy way to get a reputation for wisdom."

"You think so, do you!" said the bird huffily. "Well, let me tell you, if I cared to talk I could say plenty.

Like—empty vessels make the most sound, and much ado about nothing, and little pitchers have big ears, and children should be seen and not heard, and lots of other shafts of wisdom."

"It seems to me I've heard them all before," remarked Geno. "There's not an original remark among the lot."

"Oh, indeed!" puffed the screech-owl. He was beginning to breathe a little hard. "Then how about this one: in case of fire, walk, do not run, to the nearest exit!"

"I never heard that before," admitted Geno.

"No. I'll say you didn't! But I get around." The screech-owl blinked his eyes rapidly so that it looked as though there were two fireflies in the tree and not a bird at all.

"Still," Geno rejoined musingly, "it doesn't seem to make much sense. I'm sure if it did my mother would have told it to me as she did all the rest."

There was silence between them. Finally the screech-owl said weightily:

"I think you're a very rude boy and you'll probably come to a bad end."

Neither of them noticed that Faline had left her feeding and was standing near them in the dark. When she spoke, they both jumped.

"That wasn't a very kind thing to say, screech-owl!"

"Kind! Ho, kind you say, Ma'am! Let me tell you, if that was a child of mine I'd give him a good pecking!"

"Would you indeed!" mocked Geno.

The bird fell into a moody silence.

"Come, screech-owl," Faline begged, "you mustn't be angry."

"Angry, Ma'am! Let me tell you . . . !"

But words failed him. He drew his feet closer together and remained hunched down in stern silence.

"He's trying to repair his reputation for wisdom," Geno said; but Faline rebuked him.

"Remember what your father said about courtesy, my son. Come, Gurri is waiting, we must go home."

When they were almost out of hearing the screech-owl cried after them:

"Oo-y *tempora*! Oo-y *mores*!"

He drew his hooked beak deep into the ruffled

feathers of his breast and prepared to wait for the sun to look him in the eye.

"That *sounded* all right," he muttered distrustfully.

Geno was about to ask Faline what the owl's cry meant when he noticed a darker shadow waiting in their clearing. He stopped, giving the sign for danger, but a deep and mellow voice reassured him:

"It's all right, my son. It's your father."

They trooped in together, forgetting caution, fully aware that had there been danger Bambi would have sensed it.

After the greetings were over, Bambi said:

"The reports I have of you please me, my son. You are still, perhaps, not as polite as you should be, but you are learning the way of life. Very soon, now, you will be able to put your knowledge to the test."

"What do you mean, Father?"

"Your mother must go on a journey with me."

"We shall be alone?"

Faline said in a troubled voice, "Are you sure they're ready, Bambi?"

"You have taught them all you can. Sooner or later they must meet the dangers of the forest for themselves."

Gurri shivered: "I shall be frightened, Father."

"I wish I could believe that." Bambi's voice was grave. "It seems to me that you are scatterbrained and overconfident. When you are alone, you must be twice as watchful and ten times as cautious. Never move unless it is up-wind. Never ignore the warnings of your friends. You know who they are?"

Geno recited: "Magpies, jays . . ."

"Crows, squirrels, blackbirds . . ." Gurri chimed in.

"At the first sign of danger," Bambi admonished them, "make for the bushes where they're thickest. Beware, above everything, of Him. He is the only one who can kill from a distance. He and His dogs are the most dangerous things in the forest, but they nearly always hunt by day. Night-time is safe time, remember; and one more thing: do not, in any circumstances, call for your mother."

"Why not, Father?" faltered Gurri.

"It is the law of our kind and it must not be broken.

Later, she will return. I hope she will receive a good accounting of all you have done."

"Very well, Father," Geno said resignedly. He gazed at his father with proud eyes. Faline sighed. They were very alike in that moment, she thought.

Bambi turned.

"I shall see you again, Faline," he said, and was gone.

One morning near noon, when the sun was just about to reach its zenith, Geno was awakened by the swish of leaves. Faline was dashing through the bushes. Gurri stumbled to her feet.

"Mother, Mother!" she cried.

Geno fixed her with eyes that shone with new purpose and authority.

"Quiet!" he commanded. "Do not call."

"But she is going without us . . . !"

"It is what Father said. Lie down, now. We must get our sleep."

Reluctantly Gurri obeyed him. But they were young, and soon, while the birds sang joyfully, they slept.

Chapter Six

THE DAYS AFTER FALINE HAD GONE were filled with bright excitement. Geno and Gurri played at being grownups. They behaved always with the greatest circumspection, sniffing and analyzing the wind, peering closely into every shadow, leaving their hideaway only when the thicker evening shadows gathered, and returning with the first shaft of morning sun.

Perri the squirrel watched them with approval, her merry, beady eyes twinkling with recollection.

"Ah, me," she said, "how well I remember the finding of my first nut alone! It was, I assure you, a magnificent nut. A very prince of hazels. The taste of it still lingers round my teeth." She sucked at them longingly.

"Do you hear anything of our parents?" Geno asked.

"No. But be sure that if anything bad happened, I should hear at once. Bad news travels rapidly. . . ." She stopped and cocked her ears to listen, her tail bushing up higher than her head. "It's very peculiar," she said worriedly. "I've had a feeling all day that something wasn't as it should be!"

"With our parents?" Geno cried, startled.

"Oh, no! Nothing to do with them. But hereabouts."

"Nonsense," Gurri snapped. "Geno and I have been peering and poking around for three days now, and we haven't seen a thing more threatening than a polecat. And all the time the days are wasting and the meadow spreads out cool and green. It makes me quite tired!"

"Oo-y, oo-y!" cried the screech-owl very loudly, flying overhead.

He still remembered Geno's rudeness and he had

not forgiven it. Geno was becoming quite hardened to a sudden, evil screech just above his head when his nerves were lulled to peace and calmness.

Perri said thoughtfully, "You annoyed the screech-owl very much, Geno. That wasn't wise. He's really not a bad old bird, and as far as wisdom is concerned—well, we all think we're pretty good at something."

"At least, his being here is a sign it's time to go to the meadow," Gurri said relievedly. "If I don't get a scamper pretty soon, I'll break something."

Geno looked around. The blackbird was still singing, the woodpecker hammered at his tree. Overhead a covey of ducks flew squawking toward the plain, and a solitary heron traced his majestic course.

"It's too early," he remonstrated. "You can't go yet." But a swishing sound among the bushes warned him that he was too late.

The blackbird and the woodpecker fell abruptly silent. A jay shrieked savagely, a magpie scolded. The hare, in the pathway, made a frantic leap for safety.

"Gurri!" Geno cried.

Like a bullet from a gun, Perri shot among the higher branches of the trees.

"Back, stupid girl! Back!" she chattered; but she was too late.

Swift as a red flash, the fox sprang from the pathside. Gurri heard a deep, menacing growl in his throat. His weight bore down on her. She felt the tearing pain of teeth high in her shoulder as she fell. He stood over her worrying for her throat. She heard, as through the mist of a dream, her brother's cry of anguish and Perri's high upbraiding. Then came a sound like a brief clap of thunder. The fox somersaulted as though he had been dealt a powerful blow and fell heavily on his side. She heard, before the last remnant of consciousness left her, a strange and puzzling sound like hoofs deliberately and slowly placed. Something bent over her, something whose very scent was terror.

"Poor little brute!" said a deep and roaring voice.

The forest gamekeeper bent over Gurri, with sunbrowned face and hair and bright blue eyes. His shooting suit and shirt were also brown and blue, and his heavy boots and leather puttees were brown. He knelt over her, examining the wound.

"A torn muscle," he said thoughtfully. "That'll heal. We'll take care of that. Lucky I happened to be around."

He slung his gun over his left arm and took the wounded roe-deer in his arms. To all the watchers in the trees the sound of his steps was like the echo of doom.

Geno could stand it no longer. Almost frantic he rushed from the scene, his brain, numb with disaster, forgetting his father's explicit command.

"Mother!" he shrieked. "Mother!"

He did not even see her when she came, but went on galloping aimlessly in widening circles, crying endlessly:

"Mother!"

"Geno!" she said sharply. "Here I am! What is it?"

Geno cried in a strangled voice: "Gurri! Gurri, she . . ."

Bambi sprang into sight.

"Father!"

"What is it, son?" The deep voice was imperative but kind.

"It's Gurri . . . the fox . . . and He . . . !"

Haltingly he told his story. At the end of it all three of them stood silent, knowing that dumb agony only animals can know.

"Show me the place," Bambi said at last.

Geno took them both to where the fox was lying. The strong smell of blood was dreadful in their nostrils.

"Sometimes He brings justice," Bambi said.

"Do you suppose . . . ?" Faline said without much hope. She was thinking, they both realized, of Gobo. "Do you suppose . . . ?"

With his muzzle to the ground Bambi moved along the path and out into the dark meadow. That was the last they were to see of him for several days.

Chapter Seven

EXT DAY THE FOREST CREA-
tures held their inquiry into the
"Cause of Death."

"It wasn't my fault," declared
the magpie virtuously. "I screeched as loud as I could."

"And I also!" snapped the jay, ready to fight. He had
been accused of carelessness on a previous occasion
and couldn't forget it.

"Well," faltered the hare, "there was little I could do.
Dear me, I'm very small and I haven't horns, or even very

good teeth any more. But, oh dear me, I did warn her once. Beware of the fox, I said! Oh yes, indeed I swear I did!"

"There seems to be no doubt of it," sighed Perri. "The affair was due to her own carelessness."

Silently the screech-owl floated in and settled on a branch of the oak.

"Maybe it'll teach her a lesson," he said. "I always say the burned child dreads the fire, although it is also a fact that the cracked pitcher goes oftenest to the well, which makes the whole deduction rather bewildering."

The tomtits whispered excitedly together: "Oh, isn't he clever! Isn't he just *too* clever!"

A robin, not so easily impressed, snapped: "What are you pecking at now?"

The screech-owl blinked at them sleepily.

"I mean," he said with some condescension, "that if Gurri ever escapes Him, she may be a wiser, if a sadder, girl."

Faline gasped with hope and fear.

"Ah," she begged, "don't torture me! Do you think that Gurri is alive?"

"I don't think," the screech-owl began ponderously; but stopped when he heard a titter from the English sparrows.

"Order down there!" screamed the jay, who was very curious. "Pray proceed, screech-owl."

"As I was saying," the owl opened and closed his beak a few times which gave him a very judicial appearance, "I don't *think*—I *know*."

"You *know* Gurri's alive?" Geno cried joyfully.

"Yes, young one, saving my breath to cool my porridge or, in other words, to make a long story short, I saw Him pass beneath my tree down by the pool with Gurri in His arms. She was struggling quite hard and it seemed to me He was caressing her. This may sound quite incredible to you, but I have pretty good eyesight, especially in the dark, and that is what I saw. I tried to be of some assistance to her by flying down very low and screaming the worst insults in His ear; but either He didn't understand me or He didn't want to fight."

"Now listen," the robin said, blowing out his scarlet

vest, "I may be easy to fool, but if you expect me to believe that you challenged *Him* to single combat . . . !"

"Well," said the screech-owl easily, "I was pretty sure he hadn't studied proverbs, and where ignorance is bliss, I always say . . . !"

"Quite!" The robin strutted a few steps and cocked his beady eye. "Proceed."

"Finally I followed Him a good way toward the big nest He has built on the ground near here, and He took Gurri in. Now it so happens there's an owl I know there already, and he finds it boring but quite comfortable. I flew to tell Bambi what I know and here I am."

"Oh, forgive me, screech-owl," Geno broke in impulsively. "Please forgive me!"

The screech-owl focused a large eye on Geno. "There's nothing to forgive," he said with surprising kindness. "Boys will be boys, I always say."

Faline, as is the way with all mothers, had already passed from worrying over her daughter's death to a worry almost as poignant over her well-being.

But the screech-owl said, finally, "While there's life,

there's hope!" and from this Geno, at least, drew strong comfort.

It was hard to meet Rolla and her children in the meadow, to see Rolla's anxious, loving glances and understand how, as a result of Gurri's disappearance, her care of Lana had redoubled. It was particularly mortifying for Geno to note how Boso searched the shadows with eye and ear and quivering nose, as though to say: "Had I been there this thing would never have happened."

Finally Faline and Geno stopped visiting the meadow entirely. Faline had discovered a large clearing deep in the forest which both puzzled and interested her.

"Big oak trees stood here once," she said, nuzzling the stumps. "What do you suppose can have happened to them?"

Geno wasn't much interested in stumps. He had talked with the hare on the way out—a much happier hare since the death of the fox, and the hare had met a field-mouse.

"I don't generally have much to do with them," the

hare asserted, "I don't really. But they do get around. Bless my soul and whiskers, they go places I wouldn't dare get within a mile of. And one of them had been to His form—nest, the screech-owl called it, rather ignorantly, I thought—he goes there for *cheese*, can you imagine? Bless my whiskers, the tastes of some people! But he says Gurri's there and he says, moreover, he gets in and out all the time, so why can't she? Of course, he is smaller, you might say, but a ray of hope is always a blessing. Be sure to tell your mother. A remarkable woman, I always say . . . !"

Geno told Faline as she nuzzled the stumps of oak, but it did not cheer her up much.

"I'm afraid she might be like Gobo," she sighed. "He came back from his association with Him full of arrogance and believing that He was his friend, so you can imagine what happened finally: he died by the thunderstick."

"How terrible!" Geno gasped.

"So you see, I can't be very cheerful. Gurri is so very headstrong and impressionable."

They wandered dejectedly deeper into the clearing. It was a lush and fertile spot. Hazel bushes sprouted lustily; young white poplars shot their urgent growth toward the sun; elders, sloes and privets tangled in profusion, and a fine, soft grass spread thickly on the ground.

The old oak roots had kept vitality. New shoots burst from the tough bark, green and bitter-sweet and swollen tight with sap. Geno thought he had never tasted anything so good before.

Although neither of them was aware of it, this was the haunt of the elk. They converged from all sides when the light was right—when the moon was thin, or if clouds covered it. Geno had his mouth stuffed with the fine-tasting shoots he had discovered when the first of these giant deer entered the clearing. He thought he must be looking at a huge, distorted shadow; but when a second and a third and then a group of four joined forces with the first, he realized that these great animals were real. Frightened, he ran to his mother, but she also had noticed them. She was seized with the terror which always grips roe-deer when they see big animals.

She did not even answer Geno intelligently when he pressed her with breathless questions.

"Ba-oh!" she shrieked and ran. He could hear her cries, "Ba-oh! Ba-oh!" dying away along the path.

So terrified was he at this show of fear in Faline, that his own limbs refused to work at all. Finally he felt a surge of power run through him and he dashed after her in great leaps. His straining haunches gleamed for a moment among the lower brush; then he was gone, and only the echo of his cry, in imitation of his mother's, lingered in the clearing:

"Ba-oh. ba-oh, ba-oh!"

In the clearing the birds and lesser animals gathered fearfully to learn the cause of so much terror.

"What is it, Faline?" inquired Perri.

"Oh, oh, oh!" trembled Faline.

The hare was there on his hind legs, spinning this way and that like a top.

"Oh, bless my soul and whiskers," he muttered, "I smell nothing, I swear I don't! Or do I ? Oh, dear, what can it be?"

The robin flew down from the topmost twig of the ruined poplar.

"I see nothing," he said decisively, "nothing at all!"

"The Kings!" groaned Faline. "We saw the Kings!"

Perri clicked her tongue. "Tsk, tsk," she said resignedly, "what a fuss you make about a deer that's simply larger than yourself! They really are just like you to look at, you know, Faline, and just as harmless."

"What nonsense!" Faline bridled. "They're coarse, ugly monsters. . . ."

Geno calmed himself. He found himself halfway agreeing with Perri. Those great animals with their forests of newly rubbed antlers looked rather like his father. The screech-owl was sitting on a low pine branch aloof from the rest, moodily contemplating a bank of wild thyme. He was a frequent visitor to the clearing since he had brought the news of Gurri's rescue.

"What is it, screech-owl?" Geno asked.

The screech-owl did not move his bright eyes.

"I met a compatriot of mine this evening," he said crustily, "who advanced a thesis which I am determined to disprove. I have sat here all night, and I am convinced the fellow is a humbug."

"What did he say?" inquired Geno, impressed despite himself by such an ardent pursuit of learning.

"He made the statement, 'Thyme flies,'" the owl said with some rancor. He shuffled his feet with restrained fury. "I have sat here on this branch all night and I am prepared to stake five white mice against a grain of corn that thyme does *not* fly. My dear Geno, it is obvious that it is not even equipped with the machinery with which to fly. Look at it. Do you see even the faintest trace of a wing?"

Geno examined it. He took an experimental mouthful of it.

"It may not fly," he said at last, "but it makes pretty good eating!"

Chapter Eight

GURRI CAME TO HER SENSES AS the brown He bore her to His house. At first she struggled, threshing this way and that, but finally it was borne upon her that this creature, who smelled so revolting and moved in such a peculiar and clumsy manner, was also immensely strong. He held her easily against His breast, and every now and then He made roaring sounds and scratched her behind her ears.

When they reached the house, He carried her

through an opening in the wall and stood the thunder-stick carelessly in a corner and fetched water in what seemed to be an extra hand. Even in the midst of her terror, Gurri could not fail to be impressed by such a miracle. The water had a peculiar smell, sharper than fern, and, with a thing like a big, soft leaf, He washed her wound with it. Then He brought something that looked like a very long strong spider-web and, using His agile front paws, bound it around the torn muscles.

"A little deeper," He roared (Gurri found that by listening to the intonation she could make a little sense out of these roarings), "and the rascal would have got to the bone and that would have been bad. . . . Steady now, old girl! That's it! There we are!"

He stood away from her, rubbing His hands on yet another spider-web. Gurri noticed, to her horror, that He had taken His skin and the top of His head off. She trembled violently. The bandage bound her too tightly and the room was wholly dreadful. He even seemed to have His own private sun which He flicked on and off at will.

Desperately she struggled to her feet and staggered to the opening through which He had carried her.

"There, there!" the brown He roared soothingly. "You don't have to be scared of me. Come on! This way!" He hauled and pushed her into an open space outside with a sort of triple vine growing round it. She staggered into it and hurled herself at the vine. It did not break. "Don't like my sanitarium, eh!" He laughed. "Well, you're better off there than you are in the woods just now, believe me. You'll get used to it."

Gurri heard a commotion inside the house: a vast roaring the like of which she had never heard before. A creature on four legs with long, shaggy hair even browner than His, came bounding into the inclosure. She believed this violent monster to be a dog, and remembered with a fainting heart what Bambi had said: "He and His dogs are the most dangerous things in the forest."

This dog ran over to her and sniffed at her noisily. He was a meat-eater. His breath sickened her. She stood perfectly still, trembling.

"Hector!" the brown He growled imperatively. "Come here, sir! Can't you see the lady doesn't like you? Go away!"

The dog immediately retreated outside the inclosure, squatting on his haunches with his great tongue hanging far out of his iron jaws, his bright eyes curiously intent on her. The brown He scratched behind her ears again.

"Don't worry about Hector. He's harmless."

But Gurri did worry about Hector, and about Him, and the place in which she found herself, and the relentless vine which grew so regularly about the inclosure. A shower of rain fell suddenly and passed. In the thin radiance of the crescent moon, this vine gleamed in a manner she had never seen before in any forest growth. She launched herself experimentally against it several times more, but she was hampered by her bindings. It was then she noticed that the main stems of this vine supported a secondary growth which had the regularity of a honeycomb. She could not even get her nose through this.

She stood back in despair, shivering like the autumn grass when the wind blows through it, and sick at heart. Only one thing was good. The dog and He had gone. She was alone.

She thought she was alone until a wild and paralyzing cry stunned her sensitive ears:

"Whoo-hoo-oo-oo!"

She started round, almost falling down with terror. In a hutch in a corner a great horned owl sat on a bar, watching her with livid eyes.

"Oh, please," she gasped, "I'm not doing anything! I don't want to be here. Let me live . . . !"

"I can't hurt you," the owl answered gloomily. "Even if I wanted to, I couldn't. I can't get out of this thing. I'm a prisoner, just as you are."

He gnashed his beak with bitterness. Like the dog, he was an eater of meat. Gurri could not bear to approach too closely to him, but, as the night wore on, she lost some of her fear. Worn out, she lay down in a patch of rank grass and looked about her. To one side spread what seemed, in the vague moonlight, to be an endless

expanse of open country; to the other, and quite close at hand, rose the dark cloud of the forest.

The forest, she thought wearily, where even now Faline and Geno roam in freedom. She wondered if Geno had disobeyed their father and called for help. Or did they think that she was dead?

She began to tremble again with a violence of grief and despair. Her eyes flooded with rare animal tears. But the night was soothing, her body was exhausted. Almost against her will, she slept.

Some hours later she awoke. The valley was a golden bowl. Sunlight was spun like a web above the forest trees, and scarfs and drifts of mottled light and shadow flowed toward the western end of earth. This young day was full of a sound that Gurri had not heard before: a bursting song so free, so full of pure delight that all the world seemed hushed to listen.

Gurri, who generally never slept by night, heard in this song the peak of all the joy and love she had ever known. It soothed her sorrow; hope bloomed in her heart again.

"Tell me," she whispered to the brooding owl, "what is it that sings so beautifully?"

"That?" The owl cocked his head attentively. "Oh, that! It's just an unimportant bird of very common appearance. We call it a lark."

"Does it live in the sky?"

"In the sky?" The horned owl seemed to have the habit of repeating every last sentence that was said to him. "Oh, no! It hasn't even the sense to build its nest in a tree. It lives on the ground in the very poorest circumstances. I think of all the birds I know, it has less to sing about than any."

"I love its singing!"

"Oh, yes, it's all right!" the horned owl admitted thoughtfully. "But you get used to it. It seems to go on all the time like the grasshopper's chirping or the frog's croak."

Right near at hand a cock crowed: "Kikeriki-iii!" Another answered from the middle distance, and far away a third. Gurri jumped, remembering the pheasant's shattering cry as it flapped from its sleeping place in a forest tree.

"What is that?" she asked.

"That?" The horned owl looked very fierce. "That's the stupid yowling of the most conceited, stuck-up, pompous fathead of a bird I know. That is the domestic fowl, so called. The male of the species. You'll see one later on. He'll go strutting by here with about fourteen wives for whom he does nothing whatsoever, looking as though he was lord of the air. I want to tell you," the horned owl said, blinking his eyes very rapidly and cutting each word short with a snap of his beak, "I'd like five minutes alone with him. Just five minutes!"

The great bird lost himself in thinking rapturously about unbridled violence in the neighboring farms. Gurri looked around her. The expansive plain to the west was made up of cultivated fields, the land was a checkerboard of wheat and barley, cabbages and potatoes. Right across from her inclosure was a tall field of yellow oats. As she watched, she heard a loud swishing in the grain and several roe-deer slipped out and vanished in the woods.

"My people!" Gurri stammered. "My people, even if I don't know their names."

"They come every night," the horned owl told her. "It's very dangerous because sometimes He lies in wait for them. But they've managed to get away so far."

"I didn't know anyone came out here," confessed Gurri.

"It's the oats," the owl said wisely. "That's the way the world is. Not one of us but will risk his life for the food with which he hopes to sustain it."

He closed his eyes, but flicked them open again when a hen cackled close at hand.

"There!" he said excitedly. "Do you hear? That's one of the domestic fowl's wives. Did you ever hear such a disgusting racket? And do you know why? She's just laid an egg! It's unbelievable, that's what it is. Every day she lays another egg, but does she become accustomed to it? Does she think for one moment that she may be tearing the sensitive nerves of a bird like me? No, sir! She goes on cackling and croaking and—and . . ." Words failed the horned owl. He rocked on his perch, the very picture of resignation and despair. "You'll see," he promised gloomily, "they'll all be at it soon. Then you're going to hear something!"

Some farm-hands appeared, scythes in hand, to mow the grain. Gurri dashed about in terror when she caught their scent.

"No need to worry," the horned owl reassured her placidly, "they'll mind their own business. I've noticed that He seems to divide into two classes. Some are hunters. Some are not. These are not."

The scythes swished through the grain, laying it in even swathes.

"When it's all cut," the owl said, "it'll be my turn."

"Your turn? Why, what do you do?"

"You'll see," the bird said bodingly.

He drooped his head. His eyes closed almost before had hidden it under his wing. He was asleep.

Chapter Nine

GURRI GRADUALLY BEGAN TO alter her habits. She stayed awake during the daytime and slept at night. She basked luxuriously in the sun.

She found Him no longer an object of fear. He brought her clover and the touch of His hand behind her ear calmed and excited her at one and the same time. Not even the dog bothered her any more. He seemed to be a harmless, noisy creature whose only aim was to please Him. Moreover, the vine was between her and danger. She came to regard the vine as her great protection. More and more she became an interested spectator before whom the world passed in review.

She joined the great horned owl in acid comment on the domestic fowl. When the young rooster strutted by, splendid in his golden-yellow body with the arched tail feathers and the full, red comb she almost wished that the owl could get loose to take the wind out of him. To Gurri, accustomed to the wild, free life of the forest, the gluttonous, cackling hens seemed worthless good-for-nothings, fat and stupid members of a society of slaves.

If Gurri had grown used to Him, she still would not have served Him. There was simply an armistice between them that her flight would end.

Flight! She had her sudden dreams of forest glade, of dewy bank and misted stream. She heard sometimes in the poignancy of memory Geno's drumming hoofs, the calm voice of Faline. At such times she would run uncertainly about the corral, her black nose seeking out the distant scent, her keen ears pricked toward the life she could not even hear.

The fowl attempted a clumsy flight to the top of the vine. He threw out his chest, flapped his wings with a noise like a forest wind among the chestnuts and seemed to try to run up steps of air that he alone could see. When he fell back squawking his disappointment, his fat wives gathered anxiously around him as though he had essayed some feat of monstrous and breath-taking daring. Gurri heard the horned owl muttering in his cage, and hissing fiercely. To divert him, Gurri said:

"What happens when it's 'your turn'?"

"My turn?" the horned owl repeated. "Why must you remind me of that?"

"You promised to tell me," Gurri said meekly. "I've waited a long time."

"Well," the owl said, "I thought it would have happened long ago, but it hasn't, thank goodness."

Gurri settled down beside the cage. "It's difficult to believe I was afraid of you once," she mused. "I thought you smelled bad."

"You did, did you!" the horned owl replied rather haughtily. "At least, I'm glad you've changed your opinion."

"Oh, but I haven't," Gurri told him frankly. "I've just got used to it. That's all."

"Well!" the owl gasped. "A fine thing to be saying! A fine thing!"

"I'm sorry! I don't want to offend you," Gurri said to avert his anger. "But how do I smell to you, for instance?"

"How do *you* smell!" The horned owl drew himself together as though by making himself more compact he could add force to his words. "You smell like sour milk and grass. A rather sickly odor . . ."

"Exactly!" Gurri interposed triumphantly. "Whereas you," she shuddered slightly, "you smell of—meat and blood."

"Meat and blood! And very good smells, in my opinion."

"Perhaps they are," Gurri sighed, "but don't let's quarrel about it. Tell me your story."

"My story? Oh, yes. Well then, in brief, I am a lure."

"A lure! What's that? You don't mean a liar, do you? The fox is a liar." Again Gurri shuddered at the memories that name conjured up.

The horned owl said with dignity, "I do *not* mean a liar! I mean a *lure*."

"What is a lure, then?"

"A lure sits on a post with a chain round his leg so that he can't fly away."

"How unpleasant! Why does he do that?"

"Because He fixes it that way. Then He hides in a thing He calls a 'blind' with His thunder-stick, and when my enemies see me sitting on the post they come from all over to make fun of me and even, if they're not too scared, to take their chances at a peck."

"Enemies?" Gurri echoed. "You mean, things you're afraid of?"

"No," the horned owl said proudly, "I mean things that are afraid of me. I'd eat 'em before breakfast, that I would, if I got the chance!" he said somberly. "I'd tear 'em apart! I'd have their livers, believe me I would!"

"I've no doubt you would!" Gurri agreed faintly, watching him stump up and down his perch with every feather puffed out fiercely to its full extent. It had never occurred to her before that things that feared you were also enemies. Why, she thought with a sort of despair, that makes the whole world enemies!

"But I can't!" the owl went on. "I have to sit on top of the post and pretend I'm indifferent and they come, dozens of 'em, crows mostly, a few hawks and buzzards and a mess of smaller fry: magpies, jays, all eager to take a bite out of me. And pretty soon, as I say, the bolder ones try it. Down they come, talking a fine fight and—bang, bang! the thunder-stick gets 'em, and that's that!"

"The thunder-stick! But how is it you're not killed too?"

"I've given some thought to that, as you can imagine, and do you know what I think?" The horned owl fixed Gurri with a wide and cunning eye. "I think that He has some way of directing the thunder-stick. It doesn't just go bang offhand, and then something dies. I know it doesn't because I've watched very carefully and sometimes it goes off and nothing happens. Nothing whatever is hurt! It opens up vistas of possibilities for an agile bird. . . ." The horned owl shook his head sadly. "But there, you'd have to be a martin or a swallow, maybe, to be swift enough, and I'm not built that way. I like to stand up and fight."

"Poor owl," Gurri said softly, "but tell me more about yourself as a lure."

"Well, as I said, first come the crows. They make such a racket you can hear them from far away. They're clever birds, let me tell you, and generally you can't get them anywhere near the thunder-stick. But they're so anxious to spite me, they lose all their sense. They come shrieking: 'There he is, the robber of nests, the murderer of innocents!' Such piffle! As though they weren't the greatest rogues uncaged! They come closer and closer, wondering if they dare make a try for my eyes, and then—bang, bang!"

"What else comes?"

"I've told you. All the thieves and rogues of the air. And that's a funny thing. You've heard the old adage: 'Set a thief to catch a thief'? Well, it's true. They come shrieking about atrocities and unfair treatment and making the air safe for crows or hawks, or buzzards—whatever their kind may be. You'd think they were all new-hatched eggs that never had an evil thought, to listen to them go on, I give you my word you would. But it doesn't make the slightest difference. The thunder-stick bangs them all down. And that's something else, now. The way He picks on their sort, you'd think He knew something about their characters. I've never seen a wren or a lark or a titmouse hurt by the thunder-stick around here, or an owl either, as I come to think about it, although the screech-owl comes around for a chat once in a while.

"Once a couple of ospreys came over and, let me tell you, ospreys are tough. I got down from my post when they came—the chain is fixed to a string that's long enough to let me get down to the ground—I got down and rolled over on my back, which is the best way to fight a swooping enemy when you're on the ground. I keep my claws pretty sharp on this perch and I didn't feel too badly about the outcome, not that it would matter very much, I guess. I'd just as soon die fighting as rot to pieces in this place."

"Don't say such a thing!" Gurri implored. "You're so

strong and healthy–yes, and handsome, too!"

"What good are health and strength to me?" the horned owl demanded hotly. "Do you think I was allowed to fight the ospreys? Certainly not! Bang, bang! And that was that, too."

"You speak as though you envy them!"

"I do. All of the rotten bunch of thieves who died in freedom. They lived heartily and died quickly. What more can a creature ask?"

It made Gurri sad to hear him. Only the flooding song of the untiring lark gave her courage to wonder if there was not something left to hope for. But the great horned owl had no ear for music. He was sunk in the depths of black despair.

Chapter Ten

BAMBI WALKED A STRANGE AND lonely path. Geno asked after him in vain; his mother could not give him information.

Faline, in fact, was worried. She had become accustomed to Bambi's frequent absences, but never before had she gone so long without news of him.

Geno said once, "Since Gurri went, we've lost Father, too."

Was that possible? Had Bambi left her? Or, more credible, had some accident befallen him?

She considered his knowledge of the woods, that never-failing skill which was a byword in the forest. Could he have fallen victim to an enemy? No, it was impossible! Bambi was not to be taken, tricked by Him, or stricken down by the thunder-stick.

She consulted with Perri, who informed her comfortingly:

"No, we have no news of any killing."

The rest of the watchers, summoned for their news, bore this assertion out. If Bambi had fallen, the whole forest would have rung with it.

The screech-owl seemed to have the answer.

"Bambi is looking for Gurri," he stated tersely.

He was right.

The memory of Gobo troubled Bambi more than he had cared to admit. When he picked up His trail on the forest path and sensed its hated implications, he went resolutely on to the rescue, determined to risk anything or all.

He did not go blindly or rashly. That would have been at odds with every deep-laid instinct that he had.

Cunningly, warily, carefully, using every trick of wood-craft he had learned, he followed the trail. When he reached the end of the forest, he stopped.

A vast, open tract of country spread ahead of him, without cover, without hope if he should be sighted. He turned back from it, crouching in a thicket to consider his next move. The sky above the plain darkened. Rain began—a sudden, violent shower that beat deep into the ground and ran in frenzied trickles among the tangled roots of trees.

Bambi rushed back to the edge of the forest where, for him, the trail had stopped. For a few feet, within the shadow of the trees, the spoor was obvious. Then it vanished. The rain had washed it out.

There ended, for the time, his contact with Him; but he was not beaten. He decided to wait. For three days he awaited His return without success. Then he decided on a course which, for a deer, was extreme heroism. He began to show himself, posing where the cover of the woods was thinnest, acting the part of a lure which the great horned owl had learned to play.

Once or twice he scented the fox and, with his back against a tree, prepared to give him battle, but the fox did not find him and He did not come.

It had not occurred to Bambi yet to leave the forest. This growth of trees, of shielding underbrush, of banks and paths and hidden groves, was all his world. To go beyond its secret depths was like launching at a star, a thing beyond the farthest verge of dreams.

Yet he cast wide and wider in its maze, until one day, as evening's purple curtains fell, he found a path—a narrow way—where hardened footprints clearly marked a customary passage, where His scent and evidence were old, but strong as evil.

He muzzled these tracks and, muzzling, moved on; began to trot and, before the full import of it dawned on him, had left the outposts of the forest trees and was alone and lonely on the unprotected plain.

The path led to a house. With pricked ears, stiff legs and quivering nostrils, Bambi approached. A wave of conflicting odors came on the breeze to disturb him.

The dog Hector barked once.

Bambi froze.

A bronze statue in the evening gloom, he stood at guard, no longer a timid deer, but a thing of bold and fierce pride spurred on by his duty to his child.

The dog did not bark again. There was complete silence. The odors, puzzling, hostile, assailed him again: the strong sour scents of creatures that ate meat.

One in particular disgusted him—a carrion smell. It came from a place that was bound around with a sort of creeping plant. Step by cautious step, he adventured closer. There was another scent, he thought, dim, hardly developed in the evening air. It was the scent of . . .

With one terrific bound he cleared the thing that kept her in.

"Gurri!"

The dog kept silence. Gurri was asleep. Was she, then, already so sluggish? Was His print so deep in her?

"Gurri!"

She was dreaming of the lark, the small, brown bird that had come to mean so much to her. She saw it rising in the blue of the sky, pouring its song like water over crystal rocks. She saw it fold its wings and, like a stone without the means of speech or song, drop headlong to the earth.

All afternoon she had watched it, had known joy of it and also fear. For once a buzzard came sailing in wide, lazy circles. The lark had dropped to earth and the buzzard after it; or so she thought. The time of silence had been agony. Then the buzzard rose again.

In her dream she waited as she had in fact that afternoon. Had the lark sung its last dear song? But no, up from the brown furrows of the earth the brown bird leaped, bursting its throat, straining to clear and fearless heights.

"I am alive, Gurri!" she seemed to hear it say. "Gurri!"

"Gurri!"

Her eyes sprang open. This was another call, dearer than the lark's.

"Father!"

"My child!"

Two amber, gleaming eyes regarded them. Gurri

began to caper around the inclosure. She ran without knowing what she did, without sense, almost without volition. She stopped only when she came to Bambi, stopped and nuzzled him as she had never dared before.

The horned owl said suddenly: "Whoo-hoo!"

Bambi spun around, prepared for fight.

"What's that?" he cried.

Gurri stopped in front of the great horned owl.

"That's my friend, Father."

"Your friend . . . !" Bambi began in amazed protest.

"He's one of the chiefs of the air and he's been very kind to me. . . . Poor owl! He's a prisoner, too, and sometimes I think it's worse for him than it is for me."

"Worse!"

"Can you imagine," Gurri said dreamily, "what it must be like not only to run and jump, but also to fly? And then to be shut into a thing like that?"

"Huh!" snapped Bambi, eying the thing that kept them in. "Flying would be a pretty good idea! You don't *want* to stay here, I suppose?" There was some anxiety in his voice. To find his daughter calling a thing that smelled like that her friend was something of a shock. "You seem to have changed your ways. You were sleeping when all your kind should be awake."

"Oh, take me back!" Gurri begged. "Don't leave me here. Take me back."

"That's why I came for you. But now I'm here I'm not sure. . . . Can you jump that thing?"

"Not in a month of Sundays!" declared the horned owl.

"Oh yes, I can!" protested Gurri. "I can do anything to get away from here."

"Try, then," urged Bambi.

Gurri took a run and leaped. The wire caught her squarely in the chest. She tried again and again.

"If I could lend you my wings!" growled the owl, spreading them wide; but there was nothing to be done. The fence was too high.

"You must learn," Bambi told her, himself discouraged.

"Learn!" the horned owl grunted. "She must grow, you mean!"

"No!" Gurri cried. "I'll practice. I'll succeed. I'm doing better already!"

"That's the spirit!" Bambi said hearteningly. "Watch, now."

From a standing leap he cleared the obstacle and stood in the open.

Fear returned to Gurri. "Father!" she faltered. "Don't leave me!"

"I'll return every night," Bambi promised. "We'll practice together. Don't lose heart."

She heard the drumming of his hoofs upon the hard and level ground, for suddenly Bambi, too, was nervous. He sped, skimming the earth, for the shelter of the trees. There he slipped silently to cover.

"Cheer up!" the owl bade Gurri though his voice was still gloomy. "There are worse things than being here, I guess."

"Worse!" Gurri cried. "What could be worse? You know what you said yourself. . . ."

"I talk too much," the owl muttered. "It's a fault of mine. Think nothing of it. . . . Anyway, if your father comes back every night, things'll be better."

But Gurri was not listening. Already she hurled

herself again at the cruel thing that restrained her. Again and again she beat against the wire.

"Oh, well," the horned owl said resignedly. "I guess it's no good for me to get worked up, too. I may as well get some sleep."

He knew he was talking nonsense for he did not sleep at night; he just thought, perhaps, if he could make the suggestion . . . but Gurri took no notice of him.

When He came in the morning bearing His load of clover, He could not help but notice her new agitation.

"And what's the trouble with you now?" He asked as Gurri ran from Him to cower in a corner. He glanced quickly around the corral. His eyes focused on the ground. "Well, for the love of Pete!" He gasped. "A buck! And what a fellow he must be! Those tracks are big enough for a bull-moose!" He walked along the fence. "There's where he got in. Pretty nice jumping, I'd say." He turned to Gurri. "So they're coming for you, are they? You must be pretty important. Well, I guess you're about healed at that." He swung a gate in the fence wide open. Gurri didn't move. "All right, take your time! There's your fodder if you want it."

He went back to the house, plugging his pipe as he went. Hector came leaping to meet him.

"Down," the gamekeeper commanded, "and stay indoors, too." He flung himself into an easy chair, wagging his pipe-stem at the anxious dog. "Hector, my boy," he said, "you can't keep roe-deer, so don't start bringing 'em home as you do those barn rats. You can't rear 'em. Bucks get vicious, and does degenerate. Pretty creatures, though." A match spurted above his pipe. He murmured reflectively, "I certainly would like a shot at that buck!"

Hector lay down, regarding his master, chin on paws.

The great horned owl said urgently:

"He's forgotten to shut it! Run, child, while you've got the chance."

Gurri stared dazedly at the open gate.

"Go on!" the horned owl commanded harshly. "Don't stand there dreaming . . . !"

He paused as Gurri threw her head up. The scent of the forest blew strong about her.

"Goodbye!" she said almost inaudibly.

The great horned owl watched her streak across the field.

"Goodbye," he muttered sadly. "Think of me sometimes." And then, savagely, he let go his call even though it was full day. "Whoo-hoo-oo-oo!"

A couple of crows flying straight overhead swerved in dismay and fell to quarreling; the last, faint echo of the warrior's cry reached Gurri as the forest took her into its whispering glades. Bambi sprang to his feet. He heard not only the owl, but the hurrying hoofs.

"Gurri!" he marveled.

She was pressing through the forest when he challenged her.

"How did you do it? How did you make the jump?"

"I didn't jump." Quickly she tried to tell him what had happened, but it was hard. She didn't know how to explain the place in the vine that had opened.

Bambi said finally, "It doesn't matter how it happened, I suppose, so long as it happened. We'd better hurry to your mother."

They trotted through a maze of trees unknown to

Gurri, but gradually she began to see something here or there that she remembered.

The hare was sitting nervously beside the path toward the hideaway.

"Oh, my soul and whiskers!" he stuttered when he saw them coming. "The fox has finally driven me quite out of my head. I'm seeing things, I swear I am!"

Gurri, trotting by, cried, "Greetings!"

"Greetings," he replied faintly. "Oh, my goodness me, I'm hearing things, too!"

Faline was wakeful in the clearing. Her ears tensed by anxiety caught quickly the sound of hoof-beats on the path.

"Here we are, home again!" Bambi cried cheerily.

An instant hush succeeded in the glade. Hundreds of intent and interested eyes peered from every vantage point of tree and hillock.

"Gurri!" Faline faltered uncertainly.

Geno gave three bucking leaps. "Gurri!"

The silence all around was like a benediction.

Chapter Eleven

BAMBI HAD A BRIEF CONVERSATION with his family, and then he left to go about his business. Faline, Gurri and Geno remained alone.

Perri came running down a branch toward them. She sat on her haunches, bobbing in their direction, her forepaws together on her shining vest, her button eyes agleam.

"All of us," she said, in her best elocutionary manner, "take pleasure in welcoming your daughter home, Faline."

Faline inclined her head. "Thank you," she said.

A group of tomtits chorused from a lower bush. "Don't forget the story, Perri. We want to hear the story."

A blue jay flying by screamed, "No, don't forget that in your importance!"

The woodpecker made a sound like a roll of little drums. Perri cast a glance of reproof after the blue jay, but went on deliberately:

"We should esteem it an honor, Faline, a very great honor, Ma'am, to hear your daughter's story."

Faline said, "Won't you tell them, Gurri?"

"I'm just dying of curiosity," Geno added.

"If it doesn't interrupt your sleep, Ma'am," the hare quavered, "it would be a great kindness to me. I declare, I had a very bad shock. Upon my soul and whiskers, I really can't remember when I've had a worse!"

"I'll be glad to tell you," Gurri said in a clear voice. "After the brown He took me away from the fox, He carried me along the path to a part of the wood I'd never seen before. . . ."

"Oh us! Oh ours!" tittered the tomtits. "Isn't this thrilling?"

A flock of magpies flew in, chattering busily.

"Oh, look!" rustled the tomtits. "Visitors!"

The magpies flew into a tree, pushing and jostling those who were already there.

"Has she started?" they demanded anxiously. "Are we late?"

An English sparrow looked down his beak at them haughtily. "Ill-mannered hooligans!" he snapped.

Gurri was telling how, when He took her to the place where He lived, He first took the top part of His head off and then His skin.

"I don't believe it!" A crow sitting on top of the poplar tree spoke in deep, melancholy tones. His little amber-and-black eye roved in search of approval from his sooty-looking mates.

"We don't believe it either," they declared unwinkingly.

"Order, up there!" cried a squirrel sharply.

The crows all laughed at once.

"Ho, ho, ho! Listen to the little jackanapes! Order! Ho, ho, ho!"

"They're visitors too," whispered the tomtits.

"Ill-mannered hooligans!" repeated the sparrow.

Gurri paused until the commotion had subsided. Then she spoke of the great horned owl. Immediately a furious outcry broke from the magpies.

"Scum of the earth!" they shrilled vindictively. "Robber of nests! Murderer! Assassin!"

"You can't hate him now!" Gurri cried. "He's just a poor prisoner who'd gladly welcome death."

"Death!" croaked the crows. "Ho, ho, ho! If we could only get at him! We'd show him he can't maim our people and not pay for it! We'd teach him a lesson he'd never forget."

To her horror Gurri almost found it in her heart to tell them they could find the horned owl tied to his post if they visited often enough; but she repressed a desire more savage than any she had ever felt before, and simply cried:

"His ways are not the ways of our people, but in some things the great horned owl is nobler than any of us!"

"Gurri!" gasped Faline, shocked. "How can you say such things!"

"Oh, dear me," interposed the hare hurriedly, "is there any need for quarreling? Bless my soul, can't we proceed with the story? Faline, Ma'am, how did your daughter finally escape from Him?"

"She took her skin off and threw it over the vines and then she crawled through and put it on again!" shouted one of the visiting crows. There was a burst of raucous cawing.

"My father set me free," Gurri said rigidly.

"Bambi did it!" the whisper went around. "Bambi set her free!"

A respectful silence fell on the audience.

"How did he do it?" Perri asked.

Gurri told them how he had jumped the fence and how the next day He had found his tracks and set her free.

"He was afraid of the great Bambi without even seeing him!" gasped the hare. "Oh, my soul and whiskers, it is quite incredible and wonderful. I shall make it clear to everyone that Bambi is a very good friend of mine, and perhaps the fox will leave me alone!"

Something in the long grass under Perri's bough started the whisper: "*He* is afraid of Bambi!"

"Bambi should be King of the Forest!" another voice said.

They broke up into groups to discuss the courage of the amazing Bambi. The visiting crows and magpies flew away.

"I'm tired," Gurri said spiritlessly.

"You had rather a bad time," Faline said gently. "I'm afraid it isn't wise to say things like that about owls and suchlike."

"I shall never tell that story again," Gurri said with finality, "and what's more, I want you and Geno to promise me never to say a word about it either."

"But, Gurri," Geno remonstrated, "we shall have to tell Aunt Rolla and the rest."

"No one," Gurri told him firmly. "No one at all."

"But, Gurri . . . !"

"Your sister's tired," Faline began, with a warning look at Geno. "You'd better get some rest, my dear."

"But do you promise?"

"Yes, yes! We promise."

"You agree, Geno?"

"Of course, if that's how you want it."

Gurri collapsed onto the moss with a contented sigh. "You don't know how good it is to be home!"

She fell asleep quickly, and Faline was quite sure that when she awoke she would have overcome her pique at the behavior of the visiting crows and magpies when she told her story. Yet when she met Rolla, Lana and Boso in the meadow that evening, she showed no sign of weakening in her resolution.

Faline was anxious for this meeting. It was, in a way, a chance to disprove the thoughts she had felt Rolla was thinking when Gurri first disappeared. She walked proudly, therefore, carrying her head high, even forgetting, in her pride and happiness, some of her normal caution.

She was thinking that the children were really growing up. There was little shyness or awkwardness left in Geno's deportment, and Gurri was becoming quite lovely–except, of course, for the scars on her shoulder, which would heal. She had admirable poise, too, for one so young. Her adventures did not seem to have affected her spirits. She was still carefree and gay.

Rolla, Boso and Lana were hardly able to believe their eyes when they saw the procession of three file back into the meadow.

In their amazement they all cried out at once: "Gurri, Gurri, Gurri!"

"How *wonderful* to see you again, my dear," Rolla said, "and what a fright you gave us!"

"I'm sorry if you were frightened," Gurri said calmly.

"Look at her, she's like ice in winter!" Rolla said. "Aren't you excited to get back?"

"Of course I am. So glad to see you and Boso and Lana again. Can you still run as fast, Boso?"

"You bet I can! Want to see?"

"I want to hear all about Gurri's adventures," Lana said." We can see Boso run at any time."

Geno looked uneasy. "Tell them, Gurri."

But Gurri pretended not to hear. She ran off, frisking her heels, seemingly enraptured with action. The others ran after her.

"What *did* happen to the child?" Rolla asked comfortably, preparing to settle herself on the turf.

"Why really . . . !" Faline looked nonplussed. "You'll have to ask her."

"Ask her! Why surely *you* can tell me?"

"Why really . . . !" Faline took a self-conscious mouthful of grass. "I'm afraid I don't know much about it myself," she concluded weakly.

"Oh, I see!" Rolla said tartly. "You weren't present at the meeting this afternoon, I suppose?"

"The meeting . . . " Faline repeated helplessly.

"I suppose you think the whole forest's not talking about Bambi's latest exploit."

Faline remained silent for a long time. Finally she said, "You see, Rolla, it was the crows . . ." but before she could proceed further, Gurri dashed up with Geno close behind her.

"Mother," she said, "I can't play any longer tonight. I guess I'm still tired."

"You poor child!" Faline sprang to her feet. "We'll go back to the clearing at once. It is a little chilly, anyway," she said, looking hard at Rolla.

Geno followed his mother and sister from the meadow, puzzled, but happy to see them together again. Rolla, Boso and Lana watched them go in silence.

Chapter Twelve

ONE DAY YOU'LL TELL ME THE story again, won't you, Gurri?"

It was almost time to leave the clearing for another night in the meadow. Geno and Gurri talked softly together while Faline still slept.

It was September now. Toward the end of August there had been days of unusual coolness, but now it was Indian summer.

The trees about the clearing were weighted down with berries, the hazel bushes heavily laden with bursting golden nuts. The oak trees, too, yielded generous harvest. The countless acorns fell on the ground, providing manna for the deer.

Geno was chewing on an acorn as he spoke to Gurri. She answered quickly:

"Why, Geno, of course I will. Any time you like." She nibbled at an acorn herself. "Poor horned owl!" she added pensively.

"Is that why you won't talk about it, because of him?"

"No . . . I don't think so." Gurri did not seem quite sure of herself. "It's difficult to explain. I think sometimes that the things we value are not the right things. And then there were the enemies. . . ."

"Whose enemies?"

"I was thinking of the great horned owl's."

"But how can *he* have enemies? What is he afraid of?"

"Nothing in these parts, I think. But don't you see, that makes things even more difficult to understand, somehow. Things that are *not* afraid call things that *are* afraid, enemies. It all seems hopeless."

"I'm afraid I don't understand what you're talking about."

Geno stopped suddenly. He had heard something move in the undergrowth and now he saw a giant shape stealthily moving, head lowered as though it was cropping.

"Ba-oh! Ba-oh!" he shrieked suddenly. "The Kings, Mother. The Kings are here!"

Faline sprang from sleep, already bleating her distress.

"Geno! Gurri! The Kings! Run!"

Gurri ran a few steps after her mother and stopped. She looked around at these great creatures who struck terror simply by appearing. They were quietly nibbling the acorns. She stood her ground, not approaching nearer, but watching.

"Gurri, come with us!" Geno cried urgently. "Don't you understand, those are the Kings. You can't stay there."

"I'll be coming in a minute," Gurri answered quite calmly.

Afterward, in a sheltering thicket, Geno scolded her for her rashness.

"Don't you understand?" he exclaimed irately. "The Kings are dangerous. You must keep away from them."

"How do you know?" Gurri asked.

"Why, Mother told me."

"How does Mother know?"

"That's a ridiculous question. Of course, Mother knows."

Gurri surveyed her brother from his head to his farthest hoof.

"Geno," she said in a troubled voice, "we are both nearly grown up. I, for one, cannot always be told what is good and what is bad, what is safe, what dangerous."

"How else are you going to find out?"

"I don't know. By experience, perhaps." She turned to Faline who was peering fearfully through a screen of leaves. "Mother why are the Kings dangerous?"

"Why?" Creases of worry formed between Faline's eyes. "Why, of course they're dangerous. Anyone can see that."

"How?"

"Well, look at them—how huge and coarse they are. Great, overgrown brutes . . . !"

"I think they're beautiful. I think they're well named 'Kings,'" Gurri said at last in a rush of words. "You think my father's beautiful, don't you?"

"Why, of course he is!"

"But those great stags look just like him. I can't see why a thing should be less beautiful because there's more of it."

Bambi's deep voice, unexpected as usual, chimed in from near at hand.

"That's an arguable point, my child."

"Arguable! I should think it is!" Faline said agitatedly, hardly noticing her husband in her dismay. "What with owls and now these monsters, I don't know what's come over the girl."

"Greetings, Faline," Bambi said equably. "Greetings, my children."

Thus forcibly reminded of due etiquette, they returned his salutation; but Faline was not to be stopped.

"You really must do something about your daughter, Bambi," she insisted. "She'll be finding a good word for Him next, or for His loathsome dogs."

"As far as the Kings are concerned," Bambi said slowly, "she's right Faline. The Kings are related to us. . . ."

"But, Bambi . . . !" interposed Faline.

"It's true that something separates us and that no one knows what this barrier is. . . ."

"It's fear," Gurri asserted vehemently.

"Perhaps. But then I've found that fear always takes root in good soil. When there's no reason for it, it quickly dies. But fear does not excuse us for encouraging our eyes to deceive themselves. Fear then becomes hatred, which is an ugly thing. Only through the eyes of hate can the Kings be seen as ugly."

"But, Bambi . . ." Faline began again.

"Look at them, Faline, honestly, without prejudice, terror or hatred. You will see that even their great strength is beautiful. This, Gurri discovered at once—her eyes have, perhaps, been opened too early. This, others of us have had to learn."

"I should think," Faline remarked rather huffily, "that the scars on her shoulder would warn her to learn slowly."

"There you are right, Faline." Bambi spoke with his eyes on Gurri. Since the adventure with Him a deep understanding and affection had grown up between these two. They maintained the dignified, sometimes almost remote, relationship which exists between father and child in the forest; but underneath it a close companionship and understanding flourished. "Gurri, whatever doubts or speculations trouble you, remember that caution must be the watchword of our kind. Don't let your curiosity lead you to rashness."

Darkness now hid the trees of the forest. The elk left for their pasture in the glade of tree stumps. Faline, Gurri and Geno went off to the meadow, while Bambi stayed for a moment, watching them go.

The pathway, the meadow and all the clearings in the undergrowth were speckled with the pale mauve cup of meadow crocus. The tangled grass seemed already to be oppressed and thin with the knowledge of the coming cold.

"Those flowers," Faline said rather sadly, "are a sign that the time of ease is nearly over. Soon winter will be on us with its bitter winds and snow."

"Does it last very long?" Geno inquired.

"Yes. Sometimes it seems that it will never end."

"When will it come?"

"No one knows exactly. Soon."

They were standing, now, under the apple-tree by the pool.

"I don't see much sense in worrying about anything until it's here," Gurri said.

The voice of the screech-owl chimed in from the apple-tree.

"Never put off till tomorrow what you can do today," he said somberly.

They all looked up, giving him welcome.

"It is a fact, however," he went on, "that things are never so bad as they seem."

"Everything you say," Geno said rather irritably, "contradicts itself."

"Of course it does," the screech-owl rejoined obscurely.

"Otherwise, how would anyone ever keep to the middle of the road?"

"I think I see what you mean," Gurri mused. "It has something to do with what Father said. Love and hatred are extreme emotions. In the middle you have . . ."

"Tolerance and freedom," the owl cut in sharply.

Faline began to crop the grass.

"It's very clever to talk like that, I suppose, but for my part I know that winter is a time of great hardship and danger. I think you should live through it before you are so sure about it, Gurri."

"I'm not afraid to, Mother."

"It's stupid to say you're not afraid of something you know nothing about."

"Fools rush in where angels fear to tread," the screech-owl intoned.

"I suppose there's a contradiction of that, too," Geno said.

"Certainly there is. I always qualify that statement by remembering that nothing ventured, nothing have."

"Yes," Faline remarked with sudden authority, "and

when you add those two statements together, it becomes clear that it is good to know and understand the perils that face you before you meet them. When the leaves fall and the thickets are bare and He comes with His thunder-stick, it is well to know how and where to hide from Him."

"Something is coming!" the owl warned them sharply.

All three roe-deer stiffened to attention.

"It's Rolla and the children," Faline decided.

The two families had remained on apparently friendly terms, but still there was a sort of tenseness between them which took the edge off their cordiality.

Rolla and her children stopped some yards away, sniffing the air. Geno trotted to meet them. He would have liked to wipe out this strangeness and restore the old basis of happy friendship.

"Greetings, Aunt Rolla," he said. "Hello, Boso and Lana."

The newcomers returned his welcome. Geno went on anxiously:

"Mother says winter is almost here. Can't we play a really good game tonight? There may not be much more chance."

Gurri joined him. "Oh, yes, *do* let's. It would be fun!"

"You'll *have* to run around when winter gets here," Rolla told them, "to keep warm. Tonight seems to me to be a good time for a comfortable chat."

"Let them play." Faline said. "It's better for them."

"I don't understand," Rolla replied distantly, "why it's impossible for us to *talk* any more."

"Curiosity killed the cat," said the screech-owl.

"Cat?" repeated Geno. "What's 'cat'?"

"Cat is the opposite of dog," the screech-owl explained. "The cat sat on the mat, it was a fat cat."

"For goodness' sake, don't listen to that stupid creature," Rolla exclaimed. "Gurri, I think you've behaved *very badly* toward us. We've always been your good friends and interested in everything you do. . . ."

"Oh," Gurri cried with abrupt impatience, "must this go on forever? Can't a person have any privacy . . . !"

"Gurri!" Faline said reprovingly.

"But, Mother . . . !"

"Constant dripping wears away a stone," the owl muttered.

"Of course, if *that's* how you feel about it!" Rolla said haughtily.

Geno said shamefacedly, "Look here, can't we just drop it and play?"

His well-meant effort fell flat. The rift between the two families now stood wide and forbidding. It would require tragedy to bridge it.

Chapter Thirteen

SEVERAL DAYS LATER, JUST AS DAWN was cracking the eastern sky, Faline, Gurri and Geno arrived at their sleeping place. They had not had time to settle down when they heard hurried hoofbeats on the path. Rolla came dashing in on them.

"Faline, Geno, Gurri," she said breathlessly, "is Boso with you?"

Lana burst through the underbrush to join her mother, panting as heavily and even more frightened.

Faline looked bewildered. "Boso here? No, of course not. He left with you."

"Yes, so he did," Rolla muttered wildly, "but he's disappeared."

"Disappeared!" Gurri echoed sharply. "What do you mean, Aunt Rolla?"

Rolla tried to gather her wits together. "Why, we were going home just as usual—Boso was making short detours off the path as he always does, he's very curious, you know. I thought nothing of it when I didn't hear his hoofbeats following mine, until suddenly I realized . . ."

Words failed her. Geno said hesitatingly: "Did you hear—the thunder-stick?"

"No! Oh, no, nothing like that!" Terror shone in Rolla's eyes. "I heard nothing, nothing at all, not even the rustle of a leaf."

"If only Bambi were here!" Faline said.

Gurri's voice was brisk. "But he's not. We must handle this ourselves."

Geno stood by his sister. "Gurri's right," he announced. "We must search for Boso. Probably nothing has happened, and we'll find him looking for us just as we are seeking for him. We must split up and each take a different path."

"That's right," Gurri nodded. "I'll go this way."

Without waiting to see what the others would do she slipped quietly away.

The forest was very still. Already some of the song-birds had left for their winter homes, and with the coming of cooler weather those that remained did not seem to be astir so early.

She walked quietly, ears at full pitch of attention, nostrils held high. A pheasant broke cover and flapped with startling clatter of wings into the upper air. Gurri stopped. It seemed to her that the threshing sound the game bird made was echoed farther ahead. She listened intently. There was no doubt of it. There were sudden frantic rustlings, the snapping of twigs. She hurried forward. An old, overgrown trail crossed her own, entering a tangled thicket. Boso was there, his head caught in a snare.

"Boso!" she cried. "Boso, what has happened?"

The trapped Boso plunged and struggled. He could not answer. The noose around his neck made speech impossible. Indeed, there was no doubt that he was slowly strangling.

Gurri's cries brought Faline, Rolla, Geno and Lana hurrying toward her from four different directions.

"What is it?" trembled Faline.

"My poor child," Rolla cried, "why do you lie there like that? Why don't you get up?"

Geno examined the noose. "Gurri," he said in an eager aside, "is this anything like the vine you were telling me about?"

Gurri looked at it carefully. "Yes," she whispered, "it is. It doesn't feel the same, but it looks just like the vine."

Brother and sister regarded each other in horror across Boso's heaving body.

"Boso," Gurri whispered urgently at last, "don't struggle. It's no good. I know, because I beat myself against a thing like that. Don't struggle, Boso. Save your strength."

Rolla said to Faline in anguished tones, "Do you think He had anything to do with this?"

Faline could not tell her. Never before had she seen anything like this. But the answer came on the wind. All of them scented that sharp heavy odor together.

"He!" whispered Lana, trembling in every limb.

They heard the crackling and crashing of bushes as they gave way before his careless advance. Gurri said suddenly: "It's the brown He!"

They fled on a wave of terror, but Gurri controlled herself after she had run a short way, and stopped again.

She heard that hoarse voice as she had heard it once before.

"Why, what's the matter here?"

Gurri waited anxiously for the sound of the thunder-stick, but it did not come.

Instead He went down on His knees beside the feebly struggling Boso. The sound of His voice was terrible with anger.

"Those poachers again," He growled. "Well, young fellow, you're in a pretty bad way. Let's get that thing off your neck."

With strong, gentle fingers He loosened the noose. Boso was free. The young deer began to take in great gulps of air. His glazed eyes rolled wildly.

"Steady now," He chided him. "Take it easy. No one's going to hurt you. That's it. Deep and easy."

Gurri listened, quivering. Boso staggered to his feet. As consciousness returned to him, terror also struggled in his brain. The scent of Him was suffocating. Boso took what he thought was a tremendous leap, but it was actually little more than a clumsy stumble. At that He laughed louder than the crow.

"All right," He roared, "on your way. I guess there's nothing much wrong with you. Unless you'd rather stay here and watch me handle the fellow who dared to set this trap!"

Boso did not accept the invitation. The marvel of his freedom became clear to him. With returning vitality, he wheeled to cover. His hoofbeats drummed loudly on the hardening earth. Gurri remained motionless, her shining hide hardly disturbed even by her breathing.

She saw Him move with purpose. He, too, it seemed, was skilled in woodcraft when He cared to use it. He slid, like a snake, behind a tree. Complete silence reigned, but not for long.

Then Gurri heard other clumsy hoofbeats. Another He came worming through the undergrowth, a sly, furtive creature with a pouch like Perri's on his back. Before he reached the place where Boso had been trapped, the brown He sprang out.

"All right," He snapped, "the jig's up!"

The second He seemed frozen with surprise and fear. The brown He snarled:

"Get going, now! We don't want your sort poaching around here. I'm taking you in."

"You and who else!" rasped the poacher.

"I don't think I'll need any help," The brown He said coolly, advancing with clenched fists. "Are you going on your feet, or must I carry you?"

The poacher crouched like the fox before a spring. A little thunder-stick flashed dully in his hand.

"Keep your hands to yourself!" He threatened.

The brown He sprang. There was a sound of struggle, of savage rage, a thunderclap.

Gurri could stand no more. She bolted through the trees, back to their place of safety.

The gamekeeper loosed a terrific blow with his right fist. It felled the poacher as a bee falls when, in headlong flight, it strikes itself against a tree. The gamekeeper tore free the snare, picked up the fallen pistol.

"Now, if you've had enough, get going! I think we'll put you where you'll do no harm for some time."

They went together, leaving the forest to peace.

Gurri discovered a scene of joy in the clearing. Boso was there and all of them were making a fuss over him. Only Faline seemed distraught. Her ears were cocked, her eyes wandering for Gurri. When Gurri joined them, she sought relief in scolding.

"You'll be the death of me," Faline cried. "Where have you been? What have you been doing?"

"The brown He and another He were fighting. I saw

them." Gurri shuddered. "It was terrible to watch."

"Two Hes fighting!" marveled Geno. "Do they, then, fight among themselves?"

It was strange news. It ran among the creatures of the forest like fire through dry grass.

"Two Hes fighting—Gurri saw them; and it was for Boso! Boso's safe! What are things coming to?"

Chapter Fourteen

IN THE FALL, WHEN FROST SNAPS AT THE shrinking grass and leaves come fluttering from the trees in heraldry of red and brown and gold, the Courts of Chivalry return to the forest.

Then it is that the Kings assert their regal rights, roaming the forest paths with challenge rumbling in their throats, their eyes agleam with glow of battle, their many-pointed antlers couched like lances at rest.

Echoing these warlike cries, the honking geese arrive, their arrow-headed flight seeming to pierce the graying skies as though they were indeed the advance guard of the winter's storm.

Geno and Gurri were aware, if only dimly, of the strident spirit of the times. They heard the elk moving, their antlers clicking on the branches of the trees; they sensed the piling-up of tension that was like an omen of the coming storm; they saw the entrants in this tournament whipping themselves into the rage for conquest.

Bambi advised them wisely.

"This is the time," he said, "to take the hare's advice. Be prudent, never rash. Efface yourselves. Don't let curiosity lead you into trouble. When the King stags come, don't cross their paths."

He had hardly completed his sentence when a great stag entered the arena of their clearing. With a word of command, Bambi melted into cover. They followed him.

"Remember what I said now," he bade them sternly. "And, Faline, a cool head is worth more than thickets at a time like this."

Faline watched him go with trouble in her eyes.

"It would be nice if he could stay with us," she said wistfully.

Geno and Gurri answered nothing. They were watching the stag. He had with him five hinds, his women-folk. Advancing to the center of the clearing, he threw his head back, so that his antlers brushed his shoulders, and sounded his great challenge.

Fragmentary pictures projected themselves in Gurri's memory. She remembered the warrior's cry of the great horned owl; the roaring snarl He gave as He leaped at the poacher. Yet this was different. The stag's challenge sprang from pride, not wrath. He seemed to say:

"I am worthy of my wives. Does any dare deny it?"

It stirred her like the stories of remembered heroes, the figures who were legend in the forest. A shudder, not of fear but of excitement, raised the hair along her spine.

Faline said falteringly, "We'd better go now."

Geno glanced across the clearing. "No," he replied. "We're better off where we are just now. Look."

It was clear that he was right. From the other side of

the clearing, another stag entered, a fine animal with a crown of sixteen points and a hide that seemed to have the supple sheen of youth.

The five hinds shifted uneasily, looking first to the right and then to the left. They gathered together, their dark eyes glowing.

"Are they afraid?" whispered Geno.

Even in Faline's voice there was a new expectancy that almost overcame her fear.

"No," she replied, "they are proud."

The second stag did not answer the challenge of the first. Instead he regarded his adversary silently, with eyes that blazed.

Suddenly, as though uplifted by some gigantic hand, the harvest moon rose above the trees. Darkness had come on silent feet. The tilting ground was lighted with silver. The palisades of trees were black and still.

As though at some given word, the adversaries couched their antlers and rushed on each other. There was a fearful shock of impact. They drew away again, miraculously whole, but not so far apart this time.

They feinted at each other, glistening eyes aroll, breath coming short and harsh. They circled back and forth, legs like strong pillars binding them to earth, each seeking the other's unprotected flank. They clashed again, skull meeting skull.

Faline said breathlessly, "We must go. This is the time."

Silently she stole away with Geno following; but Gurri could not move. She was deaf and blind to everything save the excitement of this mighty battle.

They were striving now like wrestlers, head to head, horns interlaced, neck muscles writhing silver in the moonlight.

Breath seemed to be torn in rags from their heaving chests. It jetted from distended nostrils like plumes of morning mist.

The stranger gave ground suddenly; but not from weakness: it was a trick. Yet it proved his undoing. The challenger was too old a warrior. He turned the disadvantage of his stumble into an added force of charge. His great head with its crown of gleaming points swung upward in a ripping blow. It caught and tangled with the other's antlers, but the impact was so great that the brain was stunned.

A second great stroke, and the stranger's spirit broke. Like a startled hare the beaten stag turned to find a refuge in flight.

The victor raised his head high in the moonlight. The monstrous sound of triumph burst from his throat like a clap of exultant thunder.

Almost in a trance, Gurri followed her mother's trail. The trees, some of them already bare of leaves, pressed around her as though the forest itself had become a crowded place of antlers.

She did not notice the shadow of the defeated stag until she heard his roar. Resentment bade him attack something, anything. He saw Gurri moving. He charged.

Gurri took to her heels, as fast as the hare. She steered a flying, zigzag course where the trees grew thickest and where her small size gave her the advantage of being able to weave quickly in and out. The stag, still dazed, was not so agile. He finally gave up the chase with a disappointed bellow.

Bambi came leaping through the trees. He stopped when the stag retreated and gazed at his daughter. She could sense how stern he was.

"You almost paid the penalty of your foolishness," he began; but the crack of a shot interrupted him.

In an overhanging treetop a magpie screeched, "It's the King. The thunder-stick killed the King."

Bambi delicately tested the air.

"Yes," he said, "and it might have been you. Go to your mother at once and beg her to pardon you."

Ashamed, Gurri went in the direction he indicated. She had had enough of Kings, and yet, she thought, perhaps it was better for this King to die than to live on in the shame and shadow of defeat.

Chapter Fifteen

THE AIR ABOVE THE FOREST WAS like a still, icy pool. In scurrying swarms the leaves fell from the trees and piled in drifts around the boles. Crisp and dry, they crackled when the lightest-footed creature walked on them. Even the hare and the squirrel left their wake of rustling sound.

"This is wonderful protection," Faline said. "It wouldn't much matter about the bare thickets if these leaves remained."

"Do they go then?" Geno queried.

"When the rain falls, they turn soft," Faline replied, "and then no hoofbeat makes a sound in them."

The stillness threatened rain, and soon it came: at first a trickle that was like a weeping on the earth, and then a steady downpour that went on day and night. The leaves became a sodden pulp, pressing close to earth, forming a blanket that would protect the lesser plants from winter's ice.

Life for the roe-deer became a soaking, cold discomfort. When the wind came, they were hard pressed for shelter from it, but Nature, which protected the earth with a warm cloth of leaves, also remembered them. They put on heavy winter coats, not bright red like their summer ones, but thick and dun to match the earth.

"My goodness," Geno exclaimed, "it's a good thing I've got this coat. I was ready to freeze to death."

Gurri strove to get a look at her own by peering over her shoulder.

"Is it just like yours?" she demanded anxiously.

"A shade lighter perhaps. It looks very well on you."

Gurri laughed, shaking the rain-drops off her back.

"You must be growing up, if you're beginning to flatter!"

Her brother looked sheepish. "No, I mean it. . . ."

"Wait till you see Lana's. She must look wonderful!"

Faline came trotting toward them.

"What are you two arguing about?"

Gurri gave Geno a mischievous glance which he pretended not to notice.

"It's the grass," he complained. "It tastes sour."

"It tastes more sour when there's none!" Faline told him. "It's better on the ridges, sometimes, where the wind can't get at it."

"I don't believe I care for any more." Geno laid his ears back sulkily. "I'm going home. It's nearly time, anyway."

Yet when he got to the clearing, he could not sleep. He felt depressed by everything: by his thoughts, by the black, stark branches of the empty trees.

"I should think you'd need your leaves when it gets

so cold," he said to them. "It seems a shame to take them from you."

In thinking of them, he forgot himself. A watery ray of sun seeped through their branches and again he seemed to hear them talking.

The oak said, stretching himself until his branches creaked:

"Well, another summer over! I shall take a long nap."

"When I've got rid of this last twigful of leaves," the beech yawned, "I'll be joining you."

The shadow of the oak kept the full impact of the wind and rain from the poison ivy. It, too, still bore an unhealthy-looking leaf or two.

"It's all very well for you," it said bitterly. "I've got to die right down to the ground."

The sapling quivered. "I'll be glad of your company in the spring."

"You!" the poison ivy sneered. "One good gale and you'll be out of the ground—if the ice doesn't get you first."

The oak said, without rancor, "Be careful! I have a

root very near you. I think sometimes that if I were to strangle you the forest would be a better place."

"Is that so! Well, let me tell you, you'll have to strangle the sapling first. We're pretty well tied up together."

"It's the only reason I leave you alive," the oak said. "The sapling may have a part to play in our scheme of things."

"It's very kind of you," the sapling said. "I had come to the conclusion that I was just a nuisance."

The poison ivy tightened its tendrils irritably. "Don't you see, stupid, they're just teasing you? Big, rich trees like the oak and the maple can afford to toss you a crumb of comfort once in a while. Why, the forest's full of undernourished specimens like you! And do you know why you're undernourished? Because these aristocrats gobble everything there is into their own greedy roots. Do you feel this ray of sunshine that's shining now? Of course you don't! You should wish an ivy on the oak to strangle him."

The sapling shifted its thin branches uneasily. "I admit I've wondered sometimes," it muttered.

A splendid pine that generally maintained unyielding silence broke in haughtily.

"I'm not as old as the oak," it said, "but I'll tell you this, sapling, if it means anything to you. My grandfather told me, when I was a seedling, that he remembered the oak when it was a little straggler hard pressed to draw a living from the ground near the biggest elm this forest has ever known."

"That's so," the oak admitted sleepily, "and then one day an illness came and struck the elm down, so I grew until I became what I am now."

The moss which thickly clothed the trunk of the oak whispered softly. "It's true," it said; "it's in our annals."

"Of course it's true," the oak said. "And let me tell you, sapling, lightning can strike me any time as it struck the poplar, and then you'll have to give your mind to growing. So throw down a root or two, get rid of the poison ivy yourself, and wait."

Geno said dreamily, "Aren't you afraid of death, oak? How can you speak so casually about it?"

The trees creaked their bare branches until it

seemed to Geno that they must be laughing.

"Death?" they said. "How is it death to return to earth again? Our seed can grow from us. We shall return."

"That's all very well," murmured Geno, "but . . ."

A soughing sound, like the beginning of a snore, ran through the forest. It was not Geno. It must have been the oak.

Chapter Sixteen

THE WINTRY SUN ENDURED A DAY or two before a dull cloud heaved itself above the mountains to the east and, like a spreading stain, engulfed the sky. An icy wind blew drearily, in weary gusts.

Gurri, Geno, Lana and Boso shivered in the meadow by the pool. The water was dark; it stirred into sullen ripples and around its boundaries there were already scales of ice.

A robin perched on a branch of the apple-tree, his feathers ruffled, his red chest blazing.

"No need to look so down in the mouth," he chirruped. "Things'll get worse before they get better."

"I don't know what it is about that tree," Geno grumbled, "that makes everything that sits in it talk in proverbs."

"It's easier than thinking," the robin stated.

"Thinking's so much warmer," Gurri said.

"Maybe it is. But if you'd blow out your feathers as I do and whistle once in a while, you wouldn't need to think so much."

"We can't whistle and we haven't any feathers," Boso put in.

"If I had a red blouse like yours—" Lana shivered—"I'd feel warmer too, even without whistling."

"You can't have everything, I suppose," Gurri said. "Lana's got a nice brown coat, hasn't she, Geno?"

Geno said nothing, but he breathed so hard on a piece of ice that he was able to get a good-sized drink from the edge of the pool. A flurry of wind carried a scampering flock of late-falling leaves into a pile around the apple-tree.

"It's an ill wind that blows no tree any good," chuckled the robin, and flew away.

"The robin's quite right," Rolla said, joining the children and nuzzling Gurri affectionately. Boso's narrow escape from death had drawn them all more closely together than ever before. "If we are patient and careful, we shall pull through the winter all right. Why, Faline and I don't like to remember how many we've been through."

Faline said, rather peevishly, "I don't like them any better as time goes on. And now the wind's dropping. You know what that means."

Rolla looked up at the sky. "Yes," she agreed gravely, "I know."

"What does it mean?" Boso asked.

"Snow." Faline sampled the still air. "Yes, it's coming."

"Snow! Are we really going to see snow?" Geno was quite excited at the approach of this thing which, for so long, had interested him.

A first pale flake lighted on Faline's nose. "Yes," she said, tasting it, "this is snow."

Like the blackbird's first trial notes, the flakes came stealing through the darkness.

"How wonderful it makes you look," Geno said to Lana; and Gurri cried:

"Have you tasted it? It's not like anything you can imagine."

The screech-owl passed above them, flying hard for warmth and safety.

"It's a new taste," he cried. "Tangy, flavorful . . ."

For several days snow fell all the time. For the deer it was no longer a joking matter. Belly-deep, it covered all their earth, blotting out everything that was edible.

With painful leaps, Faline led them to places where it piled less deeply. There they scraped with hoofs ill adapted to the purpose until they discovered some mouthful of sour, half-frozen moss. Gradually they grew thinner. They said little, one to the other, saving their breath for the business of staying alive.

Even the birds kept a sullen silence. Sparrows, usually so lively, perched dejectedly on the naked trees, sleepy with cold.

Finally the brown He came. He built long shelters and erected racks. The sound and scent of Him were constant. Then, when His work was finished, He returned with millet for the pheasants, clover and ripened chestnuts for the deer.

Faline, Gurri and Geno were forced to wait for the Kings to eat their fill before they went near this bounty; but the sparrows and the robins pecked with cheerful impudence among the grain without a by-your-leave to anyone.

Gurri said one day, before a squirrel interrupted her, "I don't understand about Him. When things are bad, all He seems to think about is keeping us alive; and when things are good, it's the thunder-stick!"

Geno was thinking about this when a squirrel came bounding down from his home in an oak.

"Hide!" he squeaked. "Oh, my tail and forepaws, hide!"

He streaked into the topmost branches of the mighty pine, hung there a moment and swung into the willowy branches of a near-by birch.

Before Geno and Gurri could follow his advice, a creature they had never seen before streaked past them in pursuit. It was smaller than a fox, more the size of a hare, but rounder and more supple. It was black as night, with glaring, amber eyes. It raced up the pine, its claws scraping at the bark. The squirrel showed himself a master strategist. With nimble bounds he swung himself from tree to tree, using only the thinnest twigs to support himself until he found the safety of his home in the oak.

The black marauder remained quiet in the branches of the pine for some time, as if considering a further course of action. Then, suddenly, it dashed to the ground and disappeared.

"What on earth was that?" demanded Geno, trembling.

The squirrel came to the entrance of his hole in the oak. Never had the roe-deer seen a squirrel so upset.

"I'll tell you what that was," he chattered feverishly. "That was the cat. I've seen him around once before, but never, glory be, so close!"

"Cat is the opposite of dog!" Geno murmured, remembering the screech-owl's words.

"And curiosity kills it," Gurri added.

"What did you say?" asked the squirrel. "What kills it?"

"Curiosity," Gurri repeated.

"Good gracious," the squirrel muttered, his eyes big with hope, "do you suppose we could find one around here?"

"I don't think curiosity is a thing," Geno hazarded.

"Of course it isn't," Gurri said scornfully. "It's something we all have, like smell or hope. Father says I've got too much of it."

"Who told you about curiosity and about its being bad for the cat?"

"The screech-owl, I think."

"Oh!" The squirrel patted his stomach nervously. "Well, if Bambi says you've got too much of it and you could spare me a little, perhaps the screech-owl would tell me how to use it to kill the cat." He bobbed back into his hole. "I'd be very much obliged," he called out to them.

"Perhaps it's gone, anyway," Geno said hopefully. "The squirrel's getting on, and if he's only seen it once . . . Do you think it would attack us?"

"It looked rather small." Gurri sighed. "But you can never tell. I think we should be careful."

It was unusual for Gurri to talk of care, but the sight of the cat, black as a demon, and with dreadful, flashing eyes, had impressed her deeply. Faline was glad that this was so, when the cat's continued presence in their neighborhood became more dolefully evident. First they heard the death-cry of a bird and then the sharp scream of a tortured hare.

When they heard this pitiful cry, both Geno and Gurri knew unbearable suspense.

"Do you suppose it can be the hare who lives on the path?" Geno faltered.

"Oh," cried Gurri, "that would be too terrible. We must go and see."

When they reached the place where the hare lived, they saw a flurry in the snow.

"Are you all right, hare?" Gurri asked softly.

"Eh, what's that?" came a well-remembered voice. "Oh, it's you, my dear! I swear I hardly recognize my friends these days, really I don't."

"We were afraid ..." Geno began.

"I should hope you were," said the hare. "I should just hope you were. Chronic nervous prostration. It's the only way to be safe, I assure you."

"We mean, we heard a sound ... we thought perhaps that the cat ..."

The hare opened and closed his eyes with great rapidity. "Oh, yes," he said very sadly, "that was a cousin of mine. We are a very large family, you know. He was a dear boy."

"You must hate the cat," Gurri said.

"Hate the cat!" The hare looked tremblingly fierce. "I wish I were a dog, just for a minute. Oh, how I wish I could be a dog! That cat murdered my cousin for the sheer pleasure of it. He wasn't even hungry."

Geno shuddered.

The hare said violently, "I'm sorry if such a thought revolts you, my boy, but we hunted creatures must face things as they are. The fox is less horrible than the cat, for the fox is wild and preys for food. The cat kills because he has a liking for it."

"And the dog is the opposite of the cat!"

"The dog is the cat's sworn enemy."

Gurri thought: "I wish the brown He would bring Hector," but then she trembled at the idea of that great creature roaming in the woods.

Yet surely anything was better than the cat. As time went on, the frozen, mangled corpses of the forest folk became a commonplace sight. No bird or animal dared go to feed on the grain or clover for fear of that slinking shadow and those ripping claws.

Finally the gamekeeper realized what was amiss. He found the paw-marks in the snow.

"H'm!" he murmured. "So that's the trouble! Well, I guess we can fix that."

He dropped his load of sweet clover and turned

back on his tracks. Geno, Gurri, the hare and the squirrel listened to his retreating footsteps.

"Is He going to do something?" the squirrel asked.

"I don't know. I think He saw the footprints." Geno turned as Faline hurried from behind a bush.

"Both of you children are becoming careless now," she scolded. "You must hide when He comes."

"We would have," Geno reassured her, "if He hadn't turned back."

The hare interrupted them. "Hush," he whispered, "I smell something . . . it's the dog! Oh, my ears and whiskers, hide now in earnest. The dog can be terrible!"

The animals scattered, all of them forgetting that but a short while back they had almost hoped for the dog. Presently the brown He appeared with Hector at His heels.

Faline shuddered. "My poor child," she said to Gurri, "did you live with that thing?"

Gurri nodded. "He's His servant. Everything that He wants, he does."

The gamekeeper showed Hector the killer's tracks;

but in the snow the scent was thin. Hector tried hard, sniffing with his great nose and casting eager glances all around.

The gamekeeper encouraged him in every way he knew.

"Find him, boy!" he urged. "Find!"

Hector sniffed and wheezed obligingly, and ran around in harried circles. If the cat had not had an uneasy conscience, all might have been well for him; but he was nervous. The great dog at times ran uncomfortably close. The cat decided on flight. He sprang from the elbow of a branch where he was hidden and ran. Hector took after him in full cry. The cat took to the trees and ran along their branches, but Hector could see him now. A clearing stopped the chase. There was nowhere else for the cat to jump. He could not go back because of Him. So the cat set his back against the tree trunk and showered abuse on the dog.

Hector, leaping and lunging at the foot of the tree, answered him hoarsely. Even now the cat had a chance. The dog's eyes, when he jumped, were close. Two lightning strokes of the cat's claws and that would be that. The cat gathered himself to spring, but He came. The thunder-stick spoke sharply.

When the black body dropped to earth, Hector sniffed at it without much interest. Rage had left him. His job was done.

Chapter Seventeen

SOME WEEKS LATER THE COLD relaxed its grip, sunshine inlaid the branches of the trees with gold; the smooth snow glittered like a vast expanse of treasure.

Soon the pool rose as the snow melted; thaw-water cut little rivers in the forest paths. In the early mornings frost halted the rushing of these rivulets and froze them solid.

On one such morning Bambi visited the sleeping place. He moved with quiet purpose, unhurried, yet with urgency in every muscle.

"Hunters have been in the forest," he said quietly. "There'll be no sleep for us today."

"Hunters!" Faline shuddered. "You mean it is the time?"

"I think so." The great buck examined Gurri's shoulder. "Your wound seems to be quite healed."

"Yes, Father."

Bambi said nothing. He was thinking of this Him and that Him he had seen driving fresh-cut stakes into the ground at regular intervals. This activity, he knew, always presaged the great slaughter. He turned his plan over in his mind, testing each link of it for some recognizable flaw. It seemed secure.

"Follow me," he said gently.

They fell in behind him, Faline trembling, Geno stolidly trying to conceal his nervousness, Gurri almost with elation. Unlike most of the bucks at this season of the year, Bambi had kept his crown and following those branching antlers was a simple undertaking.

He led them back to that section of the forest he had haunted when he sought to rescue Gurri. He had noticed that game tracks there were sparse. All the animals fought shy of coming near Him. Even the deer who fed on the oats hurried through the fringes of the forest when their appetite was satisfied and hid themselves within its depths.

Bambi took his charges to the covert where he himself had lain. Stripped of summer's foliage it was, of course, much thinner than before; but still he did not hesitate. Taking no heed of Faline's terrified protests, he crossed the well-worn path, which led to the place where the brown He lived, and stopped.

"Now we must separate," he said, "each one going to his own place."

"But supposing one of us is caught?" Geno tried to keep his trust in Bambi, but the close scent worried him.

"If that should be, the one who is taken must sacrifice himself," Bambi said, "but I believe we shall be quite safe. The sticks-in-the-ground are deeper in the forest."

"I wish we had brought Rolla and the children," Faline sighed.

"It would have been impossible to bring so many," Bambi replied, "but I spoke with them. I hope they'll be all right."

"Shall I lie here?" Gurri asked.

"Yes, that looks safe."

"Here's a big place." Geno raised his head above a bramble. "Mother and I could hide here together."

"I think that would be better, Bambi," whispered Faline. "He's still nervous, you know."

"Very well," Bambi agreed. "Now, when He comes, behave as though you were rocks. Do not move. Don't even breathe more than you have to, especially when the great noise starts."

"Yes, Father," they murmured.

The day wore on. In perfect silence, in deathly stillness, the roe-deer lay concealed. Around the bush roots snow had melted, leaving hummocks of brown and lifeless grass. They melted into it, pressing deep down to the cold security of earth.

The sun swung up above the trees. Shadows advanced before it like searching black fingers. At long last came the sound of human voices. A flock of birds flew up from their search for food. The flapping of their wings sounded, in that tense, expectant air, like thunderclaps. Then silence reigned: the dull, ingrowing quiet of fear.

The breeze was sour with the manifold scents of Him; the sound of voices carried on it.

The gamekeeper admonished: "Remember, gentlemen, you're using shot. No large game. And leave the owls alone."

The hunters stepped into the wood, each with his loader. They took their positions by the stakes driven into the frozen ground. The beaters followed them to take up their positions.

The roe-deer did not move.

At last, from the far distance, from the deep interior of the forest, came a note of music. It was the signal horn. Close, very close, another answered it.

Immediately pandemonium broke loose. The beaters rushed to attack the trees with sticks and branches. Their voices made great roarings:

"Ho, there! Ho, ho, ho!"

"Yah! Yah, yah, yah-ha!"

The sleeping trees said nothing. Their branches cracked, their dried up twigs flew in all directions.

"Come on! Up, there! Get up!"

"Ho! Ho, ho, ho, there!"

The roe-deer could hear the pheasants floundering aimlessly about, unwilling to fly, knowing too well the fate that lay in store for those that flew. Yet nerves could stand so much, no more. A young bird broke. Ten, twenty followed it. The air was full of the flapping of their urgent wings.

"Bang, bang! Bang, bang!" went the thunder-sticks

"Bravo, you bagged that one nicely," cried a voice.

The creaking of the cart that followed the hunters was heard. The beaters began their violence again.

Geno said fearfully, "It's farther away."

Faline raised her head. "Yes," she agreed, "I think it is. But keep your head down."

They saw Bambi cautiously raise himself from cover.

"Father," Gurri cried, "how did you know?"

"Hush," he said, "it's something we have to thank

you for, really. But wait a while. I'll be back in a minute."

The shadows of the trees reached out and took him. He was gone.

"Oh, dear," Faline said, "I hope he'll be all right!"

"I don't know what we'd do without Father," Gurri said wistfully.

"My belly's cold. I'm stiff," Geno grumbled.

"Patience, my son. You must learn how to rest yourself by moving no more than an ear or an eyelid."

A fresh salvo of shots broke out, but farther away. Bambi reappeared.

"All right," he said. "Get up."

Geno tried to, staggering on numb legs.

"Something terrible has happened to me," he quavered. "My legs won't work."

Bambi smiled deep in his eyes. "You'll be all right. Walk a little."

Geno tried, his knees buckling. He felt agonies as blood began to flow through his body.

"Oh," he cried, "oh!"

"Keep trying, son."

A shout broke out from the depths of the forest.

"A fox! There goes a fox!"

Firing began again.

A howl was heard from the bushes.

"Hi, take it easy, will you! You're going to kill someone in a minute!"

The gamekeeper cried:

"Say, listen, don't kill the beaters!"

A muffled laugh and a tremulous reply: "Sorry, I saw him moving."

"He won't be moving much longer if you don't watch what you're doing!"

"There he goes! Look! Gone away over there!"

A single shot rang out.

"Oh, nice shot! Bowled him right over!"

Slowly the hunt moved away, describing a great circle through the forest. Slowly, too, the day waned. Dusk spun its first thin webs and with it, meshed within it, came peace. The cries of the hunters, the resounding of the thunder-sticks, were stilled.

Bambi said quietly, "Now we can go. Now it is over."

There was sadness in his voice, sorrow for those who would no longer lead their harmless lives within the forest's fastnesses. There was relief, too, that he and his were not among the dead.

Faline said, "Why must this happen, Bambi? Why must we always undergo this terror?"

Bambi sighed. He knew no answer.

Mourning held its silent court among the trees. There were those that were dead. There were those that were maimed and crippled who, by the laws of the forest, must also surely die.

Slowly, in single file, the roe-deer took their path for home, Bambi in front, Gurri bringing up the rear. They passed a pheasant lying quietly in a bank of snow. His metallic feathers shimmered, but his eyes were dull.

"What is it, pheasant?" Gurri asked gently.

The bird's small head was proudly borne. "It is nothing," it said. "I have an appointment, that is all."

"An appointment!" Gurri was surprised. "Here, on the ground?"

"Yes," the bird replied, "here—on the ground."

"How very strange," Gurri said. "If I had wings, I'd keep all my appointments in the trees."

"Yes," the bird said, "I always have. But when the time comes, this one must be kept wherever you may be."

Gurri felt terror grip her heart with jaws of ice.

"I don't understand," she faltered.

The pheasant's eyes had closed, "This," he murmured, "is the great migration."

Bambi paused where the path turned.

"Come, Gurri," he said, "there is nothing to be done." With aching heart, Gurri obeyed his summons. Somewhere a faint voice called to them.

"Faline, oh, Faline, Ma'am, don't you see me?"

They stopped aghast.

"It's the hare!" Geno cried.

"Yes," said the voice, "it's the poor old hare."

"Oh, dear hare," Faline sobbed, "you're not badly hurt?"

"Really, I swear I don't know, Ma'am. It's my front paw. . . ."

They found him crouching in a patch of reeds where he had crawled.

Bambi said, "What is it, my friend?"

"Oh, Bambi!" the hare said dolefully. "Really, if I had known you were here I wouldn't have bothered . . ."

"You mustn't talk like that, friend hare." Bambi's own heart was heavier with extra grief.

"Friend!" the hare muttered proudly. "That's what I told them all. Bambi's my very good friend, I said. It made a difference, too. But He," the hare's ears drooped, "He didn't understand."

"But you're alive," Gurri said cheerfully.

"And while there's life, there's hope," added Geno.

"Do you really think so?" the hare inquired. "You know, I've never had much hope. Hope's for more important beings than I. All I ever really wanted was a little peace and a dandelion growing near by. . . ."

"I'm sure you'll have them both," Faline said.

"Thank you, Ma'am. You know, I've been second to none in my admiration for you. Second to none, I swear it by my ears. . . . But now, I can't hobble, do you see, Ma'am. I'm here, and here I stay."

"That's just what you mustn't do," objected Bambi.

"Tomorrow He will come searching for the wounded, and those He finds He'll slay with the thunder-stick. You must make shift to hide." He looked around. "Come," he encouraged, "there's good cover here, not very far for you to go."

"Please make the effort, hare," urged Faline.

"I'll try, Ma'am, if you say so."

"You must," said Geno.

Painfully the hare rose. His injured paw dragged uselessly across the snow; but, hobbling painfully, he made the shelter of a thicket.

"There," said Faline joyfully. "There's even a little grass. Stay very quietly now. Don't move at all. I'm sure you'll soon be better."

"Why, Ma'am, that's very good of you. I'll stay here just as you say. Oh dear, I'm glad to see you are all well. Oh, believe me, Ma'am, I am."

"Thank you, hare," said Faline, "We'll come to see you just as soon as possible."

They left him in his hideaway panting slightly with his pain, but with new hope.

"How brave they all are when they've been hurt," mused Gurri.

"Yes, in the end, they're brave," said Faline.

Bambi was a little way ahead. Suddenly he stopped, wheeled and plunged into the bushes. Frightened, the others hurried after him.

"What is it, Bambi?" gasped Faline; but she did not need an answer. Stretched in front of Bambi lay a roe-deer.

"Rapo," Bambi cried, "are you badly hurt?"

The roe-deer slightly raised his head, uncrowned because of the season.

"Ah, Bambi!" he gasped. "Yes, it's bad."

"Don't give way," Bambi implored. "Don't lose heart."

But even as he spoke, he saw the holes in the roe-deer's breast. Rapo breathed with difficulty.

"I'm afraid I didn't learn fast enough. . . ."

His great eyes opened. They heard the rattle in his throat.

He died.

Chapter Eighteen

I T WAS SOME TIME LATER DURING THAT melancholy trek that they found Rolla. They made slow progress, pausing here and there to visit this injured animal or that. Geno and Gurri never ceased to marvel at the fortitude of the wounded pheasants. Not even the severest injury could break their pride. With shattered wings they were not dismayed in their efforts to ascend, still hopeful after a thousand failures.

"Do you suppose they don't feel pain as we do?" Geno asked.

Gurri wrinkled her forehead between her eyes. "They must feel it," she decided. "Birds are queer creatures, different from us. They have great pride."

"Perhaps it's because they can fly," suggested Geno. "How could a thing with wings be humble?"

"Do you suppose there's any place where He is not?"

"How can there be? The land finishes at the forest's edge."

"But it doesn't. Don't forget I've been beyond that, and from the place where the brown He kept me, I could see the land going on forever."

"Well, there must be Hes there, or the birds would go. They can fly far. Some of them tell the tallest stories, about pools so big that it takes weeks to fly across them."

"Perhaps it's true."

"I wouldn't know. A swallow told me that even though the pools are made of water, you can't drink it."

Faline said anxiously, "Geno! Gurri! Come here."

They hurried forward.

"What is it, Mother?"

"I'm afraid something terrible has happened to your Aunt Rolla."

"Aunt Rolla!"

They listened.

"That's not Aunt Rolla's voice," said Geno.

Bambi plunged through a privet hedge into a clearing. It was Rolla lying on her side.

"Rolla," Faline cried, "what is it?"

Rolla's voice was weak. "There's something wrong with my hind leg."

"Not the thunder-stick!" Faline's voice shook with horror.

"I'm afraid so."

Bambi examined the leg.

"It's not so bad," he exclaimed with relief. "How did it happen? Didn't you do what I told you?"

"Oh, yes, we went to the edge of the forest just as you said, but some of the hunters left the main body and came where we were hiding. They carried a thing in their front paws, and every now and then they lifted it to their mouths."

"That's how they drink," said Bambi.

"Well, when they came where we were, we had to run. I sent the children one way while I went another. They came after me, of course, but I thought I'd get away. You remember, Faline, we were saying that we had got through many winters successfully. . . . Anyhow, I thought I'd got rid of them again. I was just turning into cover when the thunder-stick struck me. It knocked me right off my feet, but I managed to get up and drag myself as far as here."

"Then why don't you go on?" Geno asked.

"I can't move it now. My leg is like a stick."

"Did the children behave well?"

"Oh, yes, Faline, very well."

"Do you . . ." Faline hesitated . . . "do you suppose they're safe?"

"That is the only thing that worries me." Rolla's eyes showed how deep was her worry. "I must get up and look for them."

She struggled, but without success.

"I think you had better lie still," Bambi said. "You're

pretty well covered here, and only rest will cure your leg."

"But the children! What about the children?"

"We'll find them," Faline assured her, "and send them to you."

"Oh, if you only would!"

"Of course we will!" Gurri sniffed the air as though she expected to distinguish them at once.

"Where were you to meet them?" Bambi asked.

"At the feeding-place that the brown He made if I was delayed and if it was safe."

"Then we'll go there at once," Faline assured her.

"Then hurry," Rolla urged. "Please hurry!"

Quickly they left.

"Do you think she's all right, Bambi?" Faline asked anxiously.

"Of course she is. She may limp a little. That's all."

"I'm so glad," sighed Gurri.

They ran through the forest trying not to notice the havoc all around them. Yet their fear of Him was made stronger by what they saw. It seemed so utterly senseless, such wholesale killing.

Geno remembered what the hare had said of the cat.

"The cat kills because he has a liking for it."

That, the hare said, made the cat worse than the fox. If that was so, He was a demon. He did not even worry what He killed or wounded.

They passed the fox lying rigid in the path. He was dead, his face contorted in a fierce grimace of hate. From his many wounds it was clear that he had died a terrible death.

They hurried on.

So it always was. The greater killed the less; the strong attacked the weak.

Lana and Boso were feeding eagerly at the racks where the brown He had left the clover.

"Boso!" Gurri cried.

Boso looked over his shoulder, his jaws moving regularly.

"Well?" he asked indistinctly.

"Your mother!" Gurri cried.

Boso and Lana noticed Bambi. They both stopped eating.

"Mother!" Lana echoed.

Boso sprang forward. "Nothing has happened to her?"

"I'm afraid she's wounded," Bambi said to them gravely.

Lana trembled. "Not . . . ?"

Bambi quickly reassured them. "No, nothing serious, I'm glad to say. But she will have to stay quietly where she is and you'll have to do everything you can for her."

"Oh, we will! We will!" Lana promised.

Boso's muscles trembled with the need for action. "Where is she?" he demanded.

Briefly Gurri told him. The description was hardly complete before they were away, the snow spurting from their flashing hoofs.

"Well," Bambi sighed, "now you can eat."

"But what about the Kings?"

"Still the Kings, eh, Faline? Well, there's no need for concern. They'll be far away. Always when the great killing starts they leave for new pastures. They won't return for several days. Until then, the forest is yours."

Geno and Gurri were already feeding.

"You don't know how good it tastes," Geno mumbled; but Gurri stopped.

"How can we enjoy our food knowing what has happened today," she cried.

Bambi said, "Those who live must eat. That is the law."

Reassured as to the Kings, Faline joined Geno at the fragrant clover.

"Your father is right, Gurri," she said. "How can we be sure this is the end? It is our duty to conserve our strength."

Gurri rejoined them. The food *was* good after their exhausting experiences. They ate so heartily they didn't notice that Bambi had left them again. He had work to do.

Chapter Nineteen

T HEN, ONE DAY BEFORE THE WIND, comes snow...."

Geno remembered how that sentence had always figured in his mother's stories of her brother Gobo.

It seemed that the snow which had already fallen was a mere trifle, a mere trickle compared with the real snowfall that came now.

Snow fell on snow.

He thought, too, that he had experienced the winter's wind.

But he had not.

The wind blew now in irresistible gales.

The snow ceased. The wind kept blowing. Great banks and drifts gathered in the forest. The trees were clothed in icicles.

The shriek of the wind, as it swept down from the hills, was like the howling of an animal in pain. Overnight the pool froze until it resembled solid rock.

The glitter of ice on the snow hurt his eyes. When the sun shone rarely, the ice glowed like fire. When the skies were gray, it gleamed starkly.

Of His kind, only the brown He visited the forest. He came with arms laden with food. Sometimes Hector was at His heels, stumbling through drifts, his shaggy coat frozen into solid spikes.

It was the time that He has made of peace for game: the closed season.

The animals sensed the existence of this armistice.

Confidently the roe-deer roamed in search of food. Even during daylight they were to be seen moving quietly through the forest lanes.

Hares left their thickets and scurried here and there in search of food. Pheasants flew freely, gathering in the feeding-place, chuckling one to the other. Robins and sparrows tangled in their legs, greedily filling their crops with the abundant grain.

Only the Kings were shy. Denuded of their antlers, they kept themselves in privacy, not caring to be seen shorn of the symbol of their majesty.

At nightfall they roamed singly or in groups of two or three, stag with stag, female with female, all rivalries forgotten.

Sometimes a squirrel, awakened from his winter sleep, peered uncertainly at the frozen world before he retired to slumber on, forgetting his winter-shrunken belly in a dream of autumn fullness.

This was a time of hushed and simple peace, in which the only enemies were wind and snow and ice.

Like the Kings, Bambi had lost his crown. The great

antlers that were his pride had fallen from him. Faline, Geno and Gurri did not see him.

Apart from this loss, they did not fare so badly. True, they missed the sweet young grass that sunshine brought. Never were their appetites entirely satisfied. Yet His store was free to them, and since the Kings had gone into retirement, they had no reason to be nervous of them.

Faline was congratulating herself upon this condition of affairs when a worried magpie spoke with her.

"There's something wrong in this wood," the magpie said.

The hare backed away from nibbling at the scraps of fodder that fell on the ground. His paw had healed marvelously. Only when the air was damply cold did he feel any ill effects from it.

"Something wrong?" he queried, taking up his old-time pose of watchful fear.

"What can be wrong?" Faline asked.

The magpie shivered inside her feathers. "I don't

know," she said, "but I'll bet my next year's eggs there'll turn out to be something."

A near-by robin jeered: "The magpie always thinks she has second sight!"

The magpie drew her head deep into a ruff of feathers. "Well, don't say I didn't warn you," she snapped.

The time was getting on toward evening. Purple shadows crept across the snow. The screech-owl sailed silently to a perch upon the sleeping oak. He sat there blown up like a puffball, his big eyes gleaming.

"Why, screech-owl," Geno said, "we haven't seen you in a long time."

"No," the screech-owl said grandly, "I've been wintering abroad."

"Where's that?" Gurri asked.

The screech-owl didn't answer her.

"What's new?" he inquired.

The robin said maliciously: "If you want to know where the screech-owl goes, there's a broken-down barn not far from here. . . ."

The hare cut in, "The magpie suspects something is wrong in the forest."

The screech-owl looked thoughtful. "I knew it!" he said. "I knew it!"

"Knew what?" asked Geno.

"When I saw that dog."

"Not His dog?" queried Gurri.

"Good heavens, no," the screech-owl said. "Hector's all right. This is another sort of dog entirely. Have any of you ever heard of a wolf?"

"Wolf!" whispered the hare. "What is it, a sort of fox?"

"Well, you might say so, in a way. And then again you might not. I suppose you've never heard of the *nth* power?"

"I never have," said Gurri.

"Nor I," admitted Geno.

The robin snickered.

"It's a great pity you never studied algebra," the screech-owl sighed. "It would have been very simple to describe the wolf as a fox to the *nth* power."

He clucked his tongue regretfully. The robin said:

"I suppose it would be very difficult to tell us if the

wolf is a bird, or an animal, or maybe even a fish. I suppose it would be impossible to say whether it has four legs or two. Whether it runs along the ground or flies through the air. Whether . . ."

"Empty vessels make the most sound," the screech-owl struck in.

"What's a vessel?" Geno asked; but again the screech-owl disdained to answer.

The magpie chattered, "I feel it coming all over me. This wolf is a bad thing. I get a message . . ." She hopped violently along the rack on which she perched.

The hare said irritably, "You're driving me quite wild, all of you. I swear I never heard so much mystery in all my life. The screech-owl spoke of a dog—bless my paws and whiskers and deliver me from evil!—then he spoke of a wolf, then of the fox, then of the enth, whatever that is, and now the magpie gets a message . . . !"

The succeeding days things did begin to happen in the forest. Again an air of gloom and fear weighed down its inhabitants.

It all began, although none of them knew it, with

the illness of the mayor of a neighboring village. The mayor had a great dog named Nero. This dog was huge and gray with a black muzzle and a ruff of fur around his neck. His ancestry was unknown, but the screech-owl was quite right when he guessed his resemblance to a wolf. For not far back in Nero's family-tree there had been wolves, those slinking, silent hunters who are the terror of the regions where they dwell.

Nero had been a friendly, blundering brute until his master's illness robbed him of his usual exercise. Cursed with boredom, Nero began to exercise himself.

Longer and longer became his expeditions in the snow, and the farther away from home and kennel he strayed, the less he looked like a dog.

One day he adventured into the forest. He smelled the life that went on freely there. He came across a carcass half picked by crows, the corpse of some poor creature starved and vanquished by the winter. His bark died in his throat. He threw up his head and howled.

Nero had reverted to his ancestors.

He had become a wolf.

Chapter Twenty

TWO DAYS LATER NERO KILLED HIS first roe-deer. The killing occurred at dusk. The victim was a doe.

Made bold by the truce that reigned in the woods, she was seeking a fragment of fresh vegetation that might not be completely covered by snow.

The hackles on Nero's neck rose when he saw her. The growl died in his throat. He stalked her mercilessly, in perfect silence.

After the kill, the howl that grew and swelled in his

great throat filled the forest with the threat of doom.

Every living creature that heard it trembled.

Nero attacked the dead doe savagely. Then, satisfied, he lay panting in the snow to rest.

The twilight deepened.

Suddenly a quiver ran from the great dog's nose to the last hair of his pluming tail. He began to hear now the call of home. Before him lay the mangled body of his prey. The shudder shook him again. Remorse flattened his ears. His tail sank between his legs.

Silently, secretly, oppressed by a sure sense of guilt, he slunk from the shadows of the trees.

That night his master called him to the bedside. Nero went crouching, his belly close to the floor. Of one thing he was absolutely certain: that his master knew everything.

But the sick man did not know of Nero's misdeeds.

"What is it, old fellow?" he inquired, scratching the spot behind the velvet ears. "What's got into you?" Then he called to his wife, "Has this dog been into any mischief?"

Nero cringed; but the master's wife spoke up for him.

"He's been out most of the day," she said, "moping around."

The master cradled Nero's muzzle in his hand.

"Well," he chuckled, "you can't tell me animals don't know what's going on! I'm not so sick as that, old fellow. I'll be up and around before you know it."

The master spoke without knowledge. He could not get up to take Nero on his customary walks. Again the dog was left to his own devices.

Another doe died.

The forest rang again with the death howl.

The third time the wolf-dog felt the ancient call, Rolla was feeding sparsely on a bed of moss sheltered by the gigantic trunk of a fallen elm. Her leg had mended reasonably well. If she did not exert it beyond a certain point, it did not bother her. She moved easily, chipping away with one forehoof at the lacy scale of ice that grew above the moss. Nero moved silently into position behind her.

Lana and Boso were wandering close at hand, seeking

some morsel of food. It was Boso who glanced up and saw that great, gray shadow slinking through the underbrush.

"Mother," he cried in panic. "Run, Mother!"

Rolla threw up her head exactly as the wolf-dog sprang. She leaped forward in the nick of time.

Her eyes wide with fright, Rolla threw herself forward with a tremendous burst of speed. Hard on her heels came the wolf-dog.

The twisting chase was against Rolla from the start. Her first burst of speed was the reflex action of her kind. Soon the stiffness of her leg acted on her as a brake.

Boso and Lana made off at an angle. The last Lana saw was her mother's desperate attempt to shake the wolf-dog off by taking to the denser trees.

It was a foolish move. The heavy snow made the writhing turns impossible to take at speed. In a race of this kind Rolla's game leg hampered her badly.

Fortunately the trees ended. Rolla bounded into a clearing which seemed vaguely familiar to her, even in

her state of terror. But the wolf-dog was still gaining slowly.

Rolla realized that the end had come. She determined on a last, desperate maneuver. She wheeled quickly as a spinning leaf. The momentum of the wolf-dog carried him hurtling onward. Rolla thrust out her down-stretched head. It caught Nero behind the shoulder. His great speed aided her. He staggered, his legs gave way, he fell.

Quick as a flash Rolla wheeled sharply to the left to cover. She crashed through a growth of privet. Suddenly she understood why the clearing was so strangely familiar. Faline, Geno and Gurri cowered silently before her.

Nero recovered quickly. He rose up smarting with added rage. The close-set privet still quivered from the passage of the roe-deer. With an enormous leap the wolf-dog cleared it. In place of one victim, four shivered before his bloodshot eyes.

In that moment Geno saved Rolla.

Quick as a flash, urged on by the spur of fear, he ran.

The others, not so quick to think perhaps, or nerveless from their panic, did not move. The wolf-dog disregarded them. His reaction, quick as Geno's, was to pursue. Brown streak drew gray fury like a magnet.

Blindly through the trees ran Geno. With great leaps, with spinning turns, doubling and dodging, straight as an arrow whenever it was possible, he tried to elude the wolf-dog. Now his speed, once matched against the birds, came into play. His belly whitened with the snow it scraped, so stretched to speed he was. His breath flew behind him like the spume from a waterfall, freezing in the icy air to tiny points of smoke; but the chase could not last.

Geno was young. The blood of Bambi did not course through muscles mature enough to carry out its urgings. Moreover, Geno, like all the forest creatures, was weak from the winter's scarcity, while Nero had never gone hungry.

Geno's legs grew heavy. His heart seemed to swell within him. His lungs labored.

The wolf-dog's legs seemed strong as tough, resilient yew, his heart as firm as stone, his lungs as steady as live oak. As Geno weakened, he became more powerful. His breath coursed through his nostrils with the sound of a summer storm. The lather round his jaws was like the scum on standing water.

"Help!" cried Geno. "Help!"

Meanwhile the privet by the clearing was filled with lamentation. Rolla sank wearily on the ground and bowed her head. Faline stood over her, crazed with fear and grief.

"You have sacrificed my son," she cried in her bitterness.

"I didn't know!" wailed Rolla.

"You didn't know!" Faline's eyes flashed. "The first law of motherhood is to protect the young. You are a murderess as surely as if you had killed him yourself."

"Mother!" protested Gurri.

"Be quiet, child!" snapped Faline. "Let this creature realize the extent of her crime. Every time she looks at Boso let her remember the price we paid."

Rolla stumbled to her feet with tired dignity.

"I'll go," she said. "Hate me if you gain relief from it. The fault is mine."

Faline said nothing. She stood looking down the path that Geno had taken. Her heart was hard in her grief.

Chapter Twenty-One

BAMBI CAME DOWN FROM THE cave in the hillside which was his private dwelling. He had been sleeping. Life and strength gave brilliance to his eyes, a spring to his step.

He went quietly as usual, headed up-wind. Not for Bambi the carelessness of winter's armistice. He tested the air from habit, gathering in all the scents, setting each in proper order in his mind.

There a hare had passed, here a deer had lain to rest,

there a squirrel had his winter hideaway. The wind was slight. The cold cut off the living scent. Yet the messages were there to be sorted out and understood.

Bambi stopped suddenly. This was a fresh odor on the breeze, strong and violent. It was the stench of a killer.

Scent had played its part. The hunt was up, but the hunt for what?

His pricked ears leaned forward to the breeze, his quivering nerves allied themselves with them. His breathing almost stopped.

He caught Geno's faint, despairing cry, subdued by fear and lack of breath:

"Help! Help!"

Bambi's great muscles flexed and sprang. Wind streamed by his flattened ears. The naked trees and bushes flew past him.

Three feet of air divided Nero from the racing Geno. Like a sharpened knife, Bambi cut through it. The wolf-dog's nose grazed his buttock. Amazed, the great dog stopped, his forelegs braced and stiff.

Bambi stumbled, fell and got up limping.

So the female pheasant will protect her fledglings from the hungry fox. Hopping and stumbling, beating a wing that seems to be useless, she leads the marauder from her chicks with the promise of a better meal. Then, when her young are safely hidden, her great wings beat the air, she rises rocket-like, leaving the fox to view in disappointment the shadow of the food he might have had.

Bambi stumbled. The wolf-dog sprang. Geno rushed on to safety.

The wolf-dog sprang again. Just an elusive span beyond those reaching jaws, Bambi led him on, a little faster now. A little faster—faster, until again the chase was on; but a different sort of chase.

Now muscles matched, and the cruel heart of the maddened wolf-dog encountered the kingly heart of the leader. Bambi's strategy, made keen by forest lore, surpassed the cunning of the dog who had spent his life by the hearth. On through the forest, up the hill, a sharp turn by a bushy laurel and a great leap to the invisible haven of the secret cave.

To the wolf-dog, rounding that last sharp curve, it seemed that Bambi must be made of air. For an instant he stopped, puzzled. Then he got the waft of Bambi's scent. He sprang for the cave-mouth.

It was too high a jump. The wolf-dog's claws scrabbled the earth two feet below it. Again and again he tried, foam flying from his jaws.

And then again the instinct of his wild fore-fathers spoke to him. Wolves do not waste their strength in useless effort. They have patience. They can wait.

Nero lay down quietly at the hill's base, waiting.

Bambi was content. He, too, had endurance. Moreover, while the wolf-dog remained where he was, the other creatures of the forest could go their way in peace.

Hours passed, watcher and watched maintaining perfect silence. A crescent moon shot high above the treetops. The Kings, their naked heads shrouded in the gloaming, began to seek the tender bark that grew on the younger trees.

The forest marched uninterrupted by the path that led to Bambi's cave. Saplings in plenty leaned toward the light the path afforded. A young stag had discovered these tender growths. Every night he came, pressing confidently upward, secure in the peace that for a season ruled the wild.

The breeze had dropped entirely. The glimmer of the moon shone wanly on the shadowed snow. Nero glanced over his shoulder. The stag was clearly visible. He looked like Bambi.

Streaking sideways, the wolf-dog silently approached. Some premonition tapped the young stag's brain. He sprang around, side-stepped as Nero sprang and rushed with leaping bounds for safety.

Dodging left and right, the stag ran round the base of Bambi's hill. It was exactly what the wolf-dog wanted. Swinging in a wider circle than the stag, he drove the frantic animal upward until the hill cut off all chance of further flight.

His back to the frozen earth, the young stag stood at bay. Without his antlers, the only weapons he had were his flying forehoofs.

Twice the wolf-dog sprang and twice recoiled. Rearing on his hind legs, the stag delivered lightning blows. The third spring saw the end. Reared almost upright, the stag's hind hoofs slipped on a treacherous patch of ice. The dog's jaws snapped, found flesh. The stricken stag struggled desperately, but the wolf-dog hung on.

The end came swiftly. Bambi, dozing in the scentless security of his hideaway, sprang to his feet with horror when he heard the wolf-howl.

Nero crept home very late that night.

Chapter Twenty-Two

GENO WAS HARDLY AWARE OF THE intervention of Bambi that had saved his life. Running had become a sort of painful twitching that affected his limbs and would not let them rest. Spasmodically, his tired muscles gathered and sprang, gathered and sprang. His mouth gaped like the mouth of a fish when it is out of water; his filmed eyes bulged.

He fled through country that was quite unknown to him: broad fields, a frozen stream that had become a weary trickle and beyond that more woods.

Finally flesh and blood could stand no more. His knees buckled. He collapsed.

When he came to, it was with a start of fear. Two crows sat on a near-by branch, regarding him thoughtfully.

"Huh!" one of them said disgustedly, "What did I tell you?"

"What *did* you tell me?" the other queried.

"I told you he was alive."

"Well?"

The other sharpened his beak viciously on the branch.

"I'm hungry!"

"Who isn't?"

They sat silently regarding Geno.

"Are you talking about me?" he asked, with horror in his voice.

The first crow hopped up and down on the branch, flapping his wings.

"Why not?"

"You don't have to listen," said the second crow.

"I can't help it," Geno said.

"You can't help it . . . !" began the first crow; but the second interrupted. He stretched his wings and thrust out his beak.

"You make me tired!" he croaked. "I'm hungry."

Geno got slowly up from the ground.

"I suppose you have to do that?" the second crow said. "You couldn't just lie there and die?"

"I'm lost," said Geno pitifully. "Can't you help me?"

The two crows whispered throatily together.

"We're willing to compromise," the second crow resumed. "It would be all right for you to wander around for a day or two before you expire. We daresay we'll be able to manage in the meantime."

And the first crow added, "Certainly. Take three days if you like."

Geno said shakily, "I don't want to stay here and I don't want to wander around. I want to go back to my mother."

The two birds regarded him earnestly. Like all crows they had a strong respect for family and tribe.

"H'm," one of them said, "that makes some difference, of course. You're a stranger in these parts, we presume."

"Where do you come from?" inquired the other.

"I don't know," faltered Geno.

The first one cocked his head on one side. "Perhaps you know where you're going?"

"I want to go to my mother," repeated Geno.

"What's her name?"

"Faline." And Geno added with some pride, "She is the mate of Bambi."

"Ho, she is, is she! Well, we'll see what we can do." The first crow cocked a beady eye at Geno's tracks. "You seem to have come from where the sun goes," he said. "I suggest that you spend the night where you are and at sunrise start to follow the sun."

"That's right," the second crow put in, "then we could find you without trouble."

"Especially," the first crow added thoughtfully, "if anything *should* happen to you."

He flapped his wings vigorously a couple of times and flew off the branch, the other following. Geno watched them rise above the treetops and set their straight and powerful course toward the west. He felt very weak and ill. His legs trembled. The place in which he had collapsed seemed to be well concealed. He decided to follow the two crows' advice and remain there until morning.

The breeze had died. The thin moon rose in the graying sky. Unconsciousness, like a black and heavy hand, pressed Geno down.

Halfway between dark and dawn he awakened with a start. He had dreamed that Faline and Gurri roamed the woods in search of him. From thicket to thicket they went crying his name:

"Geno! Geno!"

In his dream, they went on searching through an empty land under a moon that made the bushes look like tangled bones; and behind them slunk a threatening shadow, a huge gray shape with slavering jaws and a ruff about its neck.

"Mother!" he screamed with terror.

A black cloud moved across the moon, and when he

looked again his mother fled; but it was not his mother. It was Rolla, speeding blindly, hampered by her injured leg; and behind her, riding easily as though they were in some way tied to her, flew two black crows.

Geno's dream did have this much reality in it. Faline and Gurri did wander through the woods crying his name, but Nero by this time was stretched comfortably in his kennel and Rolla had collapsed with pain as far away from Faline's thicket as she could drag herself.

For all the good that rest had done Rolla's leg had been undone. Strained, painful and useless once again, it dragged behind her. She lay alone within the shadow of a sleeping elder and every now and then she cried, "Boso! Lana!" But neither answered her.

Boso and Lana were in their usual sleeping place, miserably awaiting news of their mother's whereabouts. They were convinced that she was dead.

The slowly breaking dawn found Faline and Gurri still searching for their lost one. Faline's bitter hatred for Rolla had not diminished despite all Gurri's protests. Rolla still writhed with her pain and weakly called on her children. Boso and Lana remained disconsolate.

When the sun showed the first segment of its face above the trees, Geno rose. Keeping his shadow dead ahead of him, he trotted slowly on the course the crows had set for him to follow.

The day wore on. He paused at the frozen stream to quench his thirst. A fish stared up at him with empty eyes.

There were many birds—sparrows, robins, magpies, jays and crows—but few of them took any notice of him.

The creatures here seemed quiet and unafraid. He met no deer.

Finally when the need to watch his shadow was over, he saw two specks emerging from the west and flying toward him. He had crossed a meadow halfway. To his right a small pool, deep with blackly gleaming ice, nourished a leaning willow-tree.

He waited by the pool. The specks grew slowly, driven by their powerful wings, until he recognized his hungry friends, the crows. The two birds circled twice and landed on a willow branch.

"Well," one of them said hoarsely, "if it isn't our old friend never-say-die!"

The other regarded Geno with deep gravity.

"Do you see any sign of weakness?" he inquired.

"None whatever," sighed the first.

"Then we'd better deliver our message." The crow settled slightly lower on the branch. "We've seen your mother."

"You have?" Geno felt relief renew his strength. "Where is she?"

"Yours is a very disappointing family for a hungry crow to meet," the first one said moodily. "She's wounded."

"Wounded!" Geno cried. "How?"

"We haven't the remotest idea."

"Not the remotest!"

The two crows bounced together so that the branch on which they perched swayed and a tiny shower of tinkling icicles descended musically upon the frozen stream.

"How can I get to her?" Geno besought them.

"It's simple. Continue to do what you are doing, only be quicker. Otherwise the sun may set."

"Oh, thank you," Geno said.

"Not at all. Thank *you*."

"Thank me for what?"

"There seems to be more death and inactivity in your part of the woods," the second crow remarked. "We shall visit there more often."

"Then I may be seeing you again," said Geno.

The first crow blinked his eyes rapidly. It gave him a remarkably evil look.

"You may," he croaked, "but on the other hand, from what I have observed about your neighborhood, you may not."

Geno didn't wait for further conversation. With his eye on the sun, he trotted briskly on his way. The two crows rose and flapped heavily in the opposite direction.

Chapter Twenty-Three

ROLLA AWOKE IN A SUDDEN PANIC. As the sun had crept painfully to its zenith, exhaustion had made its claims on her and, despite her pain and worry, she had had brief spells of fitful sleep.

Her leg felt as though it were on fire. Her mouth was dry. Her heart beat like the wings of the two crows.

She was not even sure there had been two crows. They had frightened her with their gloomy look and their incessant questioning. She supposed she had been feverish. It had been difficult to understand what it was they wanted. They had mentioned Faline over and over again. She could not remember what she had said, but she must have given them satisfaction, for finally the crows had flown heavily away.

Now she awoke again with every nerve tense.

Something was moving near by.

She had a sudden, vivid picture of the wolf-dog following her trail. She pictured him slinking through the brush, preparing for the spring. She struggled to lift herself a little from the ground.

Something was moving purposefully toward her. She could distinguish a dark shape. She blinked her eyes rapidly to clear them of the clouds of pain. Then her heart leaped within her almost as violently as her legs had sprung from the wolf-dog.

"Geno!" she cried.

The shadow halted. A voice uncertainly replied:

"Aunt Rolla?"

Words tumbled from her.

"Yes, Geno, it's your Aunt Rolla! Oh, I'm *so* glad to

see you, you don't *know*! Are you unhurt, my dear? Did you escape?"

"Yes, Aunt Rolla, I'm all right."

Geno broke through to the spot where she lay. She looked at him anxiously.

"Geno, you're not angry with me, too?"

"Angry? Why should I be? But why are you lying here? Aren't you well?"

In her great relief, she felt capable of anything. With a supreme effort she struggled to her feet.

"Of *course* I'm all right, Geno. There, you see? My stupid old leg was bothering me a little. But let's go to your mother at *once*. Poor dear, she's quite beside herself."

"The crows said she was here, but they must have meant you."

"The crows? Oh, how stupid of me! I'm afraid I've given you a great deal of trouble."

A large jay lighted on a twig above them. "Geno!" he shrieked in loud surprise. "Well, I never did!"

"Never did what?" Geno inquired.

The magpie joined the jay.

"I knew it!" she piped. "I knew it! I knew it!"

"How do you do?" Geno said politely.

"Do what?" screamed the jay. "There you are, you see. Other people can ask stupid questions too."

"Your mother is looking for you, Geno," the magpie said. "She's quite frantic."

Rolla said anxiously, "Perhaps one of you knows where my children are."

"Oh, yes," the jay assured her. "They're waiting for you where you live."

The magpie said in a high dreamy voice, "I get a message!"

Geno said, "I hope it's about my mother."

The magpie rocked back and forward on the twig. "I see somebody searching. There are two roe-deer. They are Faline and her daughter."

The jay said impatiently, "I could have told you that."

The magpie peered furtively through the trees. "I see them coming nearer. They are coming this way. . . ."

"Faline!" cried Rolla.

They all heard the rustling near at hand. With Rolla's cry it stopped.

"Yes, Aunt Rolla?" Gurri's voice answered.

They heard Faline say harshly:

"Gurri, I forbid you to speak to her. I forbid it, do you hear?"

"But, Faline," Rolla said, "Geno has returned. I have found him. He is here."

There was complete silence until Geno spoke.

"Yes, Mother, it is I."

Then Faline cried in a breaking voice, "Geno! Oh, it can't be!"

They heard the sound of careless, rushing approach. Faline stumbled into the thicket.

"Mother!" Geno cried.

Rolla murmured softly, " I must go to *my* children."

Happiness is sometimes very selfish. Faline, Gurri and Geno hardly noticed her as she limped painfully away.

Gurri was trying to dance in spite of being tangled in twigs and branches.

"Geno," she demanded, "how did you manage it? How did you escape?"

Geno replied loftily, "Huh, it was nothing! I fooled the wolf-dog."

"I don't believe it," Gurri cried. "I'll bet . . ." She paused and then said breathlessly, "I'll bet Father was somewhere near."

"Well . . ." Geno began.

"He was, wasn't he?"

"Well, yes."

"How is he?" Faline demanded eagerly.

Although at the time Geno had not seemed to realize what Bambi had done for him, these questions took a cover off his memory.

"Oh, you should have seen him," he cried enthusiastically. "He came like the wind between the wolf-dog and me, and then . . ."

They listened eagerly to his story.

"What terrible creatures!" Faline shuddered when he told about the crows.

"Birds *are* funny," Gurri mused. She was thinking

again about the great horned owl. "They talk so unpleas-
antly and they act so kindly."

Faline sighed. "Well," she said, "you've had a terrible
experience, and you're so young to face it alone."

"Has the wolf-dog been seen again?" Geno asked.

"The birds say . . ." Faline faltered. "They say he killed
a young Prince."

"What will we do if he comes back?"

"I don't know. We mustn't think of it."

"Poor Rolla," Gurri said suddenly.

"Where did she go?" Geno asked.

Faline said nothing. She knew that it was ungenerous,
but she could not yet forget that it was Rolla who had put
Geno in danger by leading the wolf-dog to their clearing.

"Can't we be friends again?" pleaded Gurri. "After
all, she was frightened and in pain. She didn't know
what she was doing."

"Why are you angry with Aunt Rolla?" Geno
inquired, puzzled.

"It doesn't matter, my son," Faline answered in a
muffled voice.

"But it does, Mother," Gurri cried.

"I shall have to think," Faline muttered. "She broke the first law of the forest by leading an enemy against her kind."

"But she didn't mean to. And Geno is safe. Let's visit her."

"Very well," Faline agreed reluctantly.

Gurri skipped out of the thicket.

"Come on, then. Let's go quickly!"

They trotted toward Rolla's sleeping place, Faline and Geno very close together, Gurri leading. There they interrupted another scene of joy.

Rolla lay exhausted, in pain but happy, while Boso and Lana stood close to her telling her all they had been doing; but when Faline, Geno and Gurri appeared an uneasy silence fell upon the group.

"Well?" Boso said distantly.

"How are you, Aunt Rolla?" Gurri spoke cheerily, trying to overcome the too apparent strain.

"She's very well, thank you," replied Boso inaccurately. He eyed Geno with subdued antagonism. Lana burst out:

"We're so glad you're all right, Geno."

Geno dug at the snow with his forehoof.

"Well . . ." he began; but Boso interrupted him.

"Quite the hero, aren't you!"

"What is the matter with you all?" Gurri said impatiently.

"The matter with us?" Boso's lip curled. "We're grateful to Geno for saving Mother's life."

Faline burst in angrily, "You should be!"

"We are," Boso said with false heartiness.

"Must we go on like this?" Lana put in tearfully. "It's all a misunderstanding. We know Mother wouldn't wish Geno any harm."

"Look at her," said Boso. "She looks dangerous, doesn't she! She can't even move."

"I don't like your attitude, Boso," Faline snapped.

"I'm sorry. But I should have thought the least you could do was to send a messenger to tell us she was injured, instead of driving her away."

"Boso!" wailed Rolla. "Don't behave like that!"

"You can't blame him," Gurri said. "It was unkind of us.

"Unkind," burst in Faline, "when she . . ."

"I think we'd better go," Geno said soberly.

"Geno!" Lana cried. "I'm sure it'll all come right!"

But despite Lana's protests, there was a barrier between the two families, and all chance of ending it then and there passed when a far-off crashing was heard among the trees. At the same time a cheerful whistling disturbed the air.

"*He!*" whispered Faline fearfully.

Immediately the roe-deer turned and vanished.

The gamekeeper went plodding along the path, the thunder-stick slung over his left arm, whistling gaily. He scanned the trees and the ground with keen eyes, his high boots grinding in the snow.

Soon he came to the hill where Bambi had his cave. Bambi was there, but he remained very quiet when he heard, saw and smelled Him.

Having skirted the hill, the gamekeeper stopped abruptly. He had found the torn carcass of Nero's victim.

"Here, now, what the dickens is this?" he muttered.

He cast around carefully, examining the corpse and

the scene of battle. Tangled in a bush he found a few gray hairs. Paw-prints were easy to discern.

"A wolf!" he exclaimed, bewildered. "In these parts!"

Abruptly light came to him. He slapped his knee.

"The mayor's dog Nero! He's become a killer!"

The gamekeeper looked very grim and absorbed as he followed the wolf-dog's tracks. He came to the verge of the forest.

"Well," he said to himself, "that dog is going to get a shock, I'm afraid."

He fumbled in his pockets and drew out a couple of cartridges. They contained the smallest size shot and would not kill the dog; but they would pepper his hide in a way he would not easily forget.

Patiently he lurked in hiding. Nero did not come. During the next two days, the gamekeeper went back to the spot early and waited for Nero; but the dog did not return.

On the third day he saw a shadow skulking under the hedgerow; but if it was Nero the wind carried the human scent to him, and he turned back.

The fifth day came. In mid-afternoon, the game-keeper glanced over his shoulder. Bambi stood at the foot of his hill, head held high, sniffing the air.

"Glory be!" the gamekeeper murmured. "What an animal! I hope I see him later on when he has his points."

Something diverted his attention, and when he looked again, Bambi was gone. He gazed around. It was, he thought, a remarkable disappearance. The entrance to the cave was not visible to him. Then he saw again that stalking shadow in the hedgerow. He cocked his gun.

Today the air was right. Nero had no suspicion that he was being watched. He trotted swiftly from shadow to shadow, red eyes searching for game. A hare sprang out. Normally Nero would not have bothered with anything so insignificant as a hare. He had developed richer tastes. This afternoon, however, he was bored. He took off after the hare without thinking.

The hare ran directly toward Bambi's hill, his terrified ears flat on his back, his cotton-tail gleaming whitely. He tore past without even scenting Him, and Nero flashed along close behind.

The gamekeeper had followed the wolf-dog's course with the shifting barrels of his gun. One after the other, he fired them into the racing animal's rump. Nero spun round howling with pain. The gamekeeper rose threateningly.

"Let that be a lesson to you," he roared.

The great dog cowered. Again he remembered the appalling fact that He knew everything. His ears drooped. His tail curled between his legs.

"Get home with you!"

Nero whimpered pitiably. Dejectedly, oppressed now with a dreadful sense of guilt, he limped down the incline toward home. Impelled by His scolding voice and the sparkling pain that tormented his rump, he broke into a painful trot. He felt that if a deer should show itself he would faint with mortification; but none did.

The gamekeeper followed more slowly. The mayor

was by this time getting well, and he found him sitting comfortably in an easy chair. He made his report.

"Why, the ungrateful brute! Come here, sir!" bellowed the mayor.

From Nero's point of view, the worst had happened. There was no further pit of shame into which he could sink. He approached the dread presence mournfully.

"You should have been shot outright," the mayor shouted. "Outright, do you hear? You have to thank the gamekeeper for giving you a second chance."

The repentant dog tried to lick his master's hand.

"Don't make up to me, sir! Get to your kennel!"

The gamekeeper laughed.

"I guess he's learned his lesson," he said.

"I hope so!" the mayor said fervently. "I'd hate to lose that dog. Why, when I was very sick, he knew more about me than the doctor."

"He's a handsome animal," the gamekeeper murmured diplomatically.

"Well, no matter!" The mayor offered his tobacco. "If

you catch him at it again, there's only one thing to do. I won't be responsible for a killer."

The gamekeeper tamped tobacco into a well-colored briar. He hoped that Nero would now behave himself. Probably he would, once his master was up and about again.

Chapter Twenty-Four

IN THE FOREST, DAYS OF PEACE SUC-
ceeded the terror the wolf-dog had caused. The
weather grew noticeably milder. There were days
when the sky was a pale wash of blue without a
cloud. A white sun shone, powerless but cheerful.

One day Geno called to his mother.

"Look," he said wonderingly, "the snow has flowers!"

Faline looked. The ground was thick with snowdrops.

"Yes," she told him comfortably, "that means the
snow will soon be gone."

"You mean, the cold is going? The meadow will be green again?"

"Yes. Good times are coming."

"Oh," cried Gurri, "imagine being able to romp again!"

"It will be fun!" admitted Geno, examining the snow anxiously to see if he could notice it going.

Soon the sun gained power. The forest was filled with the tinkle of running water. The ground grew soft and marshy underfoot. In the meadow the pool swelled until the whole field was a lake of water.

"My goodness," Geno grumbled, regarding his reflection in it, "this isn't much fun!"

"It must be fun for the fish," Gurri said.

"Well, I'm not a fish!" Geno turned away with disgust.

"It will pass," Faline assured him, "and the grass will be greener for it."

"Well, that's a comfort," Geno said, leading the way back to the clearing.

A squirrel was sitting outside his hole in the oak,

blinking his eyes after his long hibernation. His stomach rumbled from his long fast.

"Oh, pardon me!" he muttered. A drop of melting water fell and hit him on the nose.

"You look thin, squirrel," Gurri said.

"Thin! My vest positively hangs on me!" He looked around hungrily. "If I could only remember where I put those nuts." He looked suspiciously at Geno as though he suspected him of stealing his stores. "I suppose I'll have to come down and start searching. It's the same every year."

"You should learn to remember," said Gurri.

"Learn to remember!" snapped the squirrel. "It's all anyone can do to remember to learn, if you ask me." He went back into his hole, wagging his head from side to side, his tail bushy with indignation.

Geno grew more impatient. "Now it's started to rain!"

It had. The sky had suddenly darkened. The rain changed from a shower to a steady downpour.

"The fish will go crazy with happiness if this keeps up," Geno grumbled, "but I shall only go crazy!"

"Be patient," Faline advised him.

"Patient!" repeated Geno sulkily.

"Dear me," Faline groaned, "you whine just as you did when you were little. Remember you're supposed to be growing up. You've had your adventures. You've faced great dangers. Try to be like your father."

"Where is Father?" Geno inquired. "It's long enough since we've seen him."

"He'll be coming."

"The sun will be coming, the grass will be coming, Father will be coming! It's likely to be pretty busy hereabout if they all come at once."

The storm changed to a rattle of thunder, drowning out his words. The wind rose. Geno took shelter under the oak. Its branches groaned. Suddenly one of them parted from the trunk and crashed to the ground. Geno started up with fear, but the branch formed an additional barrier against the storm and he soon was glad to avail himself of the shelter. He began to doze, despite the raging of the wind and the loud torment of the trees.

The oak cried, "Well, this is a rude awakening! How was the winter, pine?"

"Fair enough," the pine replied. "You certainly slept well."

The oak stretched creakingly. "I seem to have lost a branch. I thought I felt something go. Hi, sapling!"

"Yes, sir!" answered the sapling respectfully.

"That's right," applauded the oak. "Always wake up promptly. Now, what was I going to say?"

"I don't know, sir."

The oak groaned a little as though from the effort of thinking.

"Oh, yes," he said, "I've lost a branch. I'm glad to see it was right above you. You can grow better now."

"I certainly shall," said the sapling thankfully.

The maple yawned and broke into the conversation. "You'd better talk less and hold on more if you want to last this storm out," he advised.

Indeed, at that moment, a blast of wind hit the sapling that bent it double. All the trees preserved silence, and only the lashing of their branches and the straining of their mighty trunks were heard.

Geno awoke.

"I wish the trees would talk sometimes when I'm fully awake," he murmured. "There are a couple of questions I'd like to ask. A couple of questions!" he repeated hopefully in a loud voice; but the trees took no notice of him.

With morning the storm died down. The rain had carried nearly all the snow away, and the wind had dried the heights. A friendly sun greeted the pheasants as, with cries of joy, they left their sleeping places.

Spring had arrived on the wings of the storm.

A blackbird already rehearsed his song in the top-most branches of a maple. Magpies exchanged their gossip with renewed vigor, chasing each other through the branches of the trees, and jays sat sunning themselves and making spiteful comments about their neighbors.

Next day came the call to labor. The air was full of hurrying birds carrying wisps of grass or hay or straw to use in building their nests. Others fluttered around their homes to consider the winter's damages, patching here, smoothing a little mud there, trying to avoid the serious labor of new construction.

Faline, Gurri and Geno, free of such activity, sunned themselves sleepily. Geno's head was nodding when Faline briskly said:

"Children, we really shouldn't waste time here when so much is going on. At least we could go and get some exercise."

"What sort of exercise?" Geno demanded.

"Well, the flood is down in the meadow. You could have a good romp there."

"In daylight?" Geno was surprised.

"Oh, yes, it's quite safe at this season of the year."

"I'd love it!" Gurri cried with enthusiasm.

"Let's go then."

The three roe-deer arose and trotted along the path to the meadow.

Suddenly Gurri stopped.

"Mother!" she exclaimed with awe. "Look at the top of Geno's head!"

Geno almost turned his eyes over backward trying to see it.

"What's the matter with it?" He felt an itch now because his attention had been drawn to it. He rubbed it on a tree.

"It's got bumps on it!" Gurri said.

Faline chuckled deep in her throat, but Geno was worried.

"Bumps!" Once again Geno tried to perform the impossible feat of surveying the top of his head. "Is something wrong with me?"

"Maybe you've been bitten."

"Children!" Faline said with amusement in her voice. "Don't you see, Geno is growing up. Those are the beginnings of his antlers."

"Antlers! You mean I'm going to have a crown?"

"Of course you are, son! Just like your father's. Just as handsome, perhaps."

Geno strutted along the path, his legs stiff, his head held high.

"Oh, Mother, a crown!"

"Your father looked just like you when he was young," Faline told him wistfully.

Gurri feigned horror. "Don't flatter him so much. He'll burst. Maybe those bumps are only vanity coming out."

Geno was too pleased to be offended. He frisked up and down the path, shouting:

"I'm going to have a crown! I'm going to have a crown!"

When they came to the meadow, he rushed to look at himself in the pool. The water made his face look long and rather peculiar. He had hoped to see something on his head as long and sharp as a fork of lightning. To his disappointment, he could discern nothing.

"I don't see anything," he said in an aggrieved tone.

"Nevertheless, your crown is coming," Faline assured him.

The serious way in which she spoke made him happy again.

Shortly Rolla, Lana and Boso arrived.

This was the first time the two families had met since the unpleasant episode which followed Geno's return from his adventure with the wolf-dog. Time had strengthened, rather than dispelled, the discord. Geno and Boso regarded each other with antagonism.

Gurri was still disturbed about this state of affairs. She desired, above almost everything else, the restoration of their old, pleasant comradeship. In this she felt she had an ally in Lana. She hurried forward, crying:

"Lana, look! Geno's getting his crown!"

"I hope it fits *his majesty*!" said Boso sourly.

Geno said nothing. He was scanning Boso's head with great anxiety to discover if, perhaps, Boso had more apparent bumps than he. But Boso's head appeared quite smooth and natural.

"Maybe you'd better grow up before you say anything," he said.

"It's normal for you to have a swelled head," Boso replied.

"Please, Boso and Geno!" Gurri said.

Lana kept silent. Geno and Boso looked at each other with expressions which they imagined to be of the greatest ferocity. At last Lana laughed. "You don't know how funny you look, Geno," she said.

"Funny!" Geno rasped.

"Making faces like that, I mean."

"Oh, so I'm making faces, am I! Well, let me tell you, you have the funniest face I ever saw . . . except Boso's," Geno added as an afterthought.

Lana gasped. "Why, you rude boy . . . !"

Rolla said, "Children, please!" and looked beseechingly at Faline.

Faline, however, did not intervene. Ever since Boso had suggested that it was cruel of her to drive Rolla away when she was hurt instead of sending a message to her children, she had suspected that she might not be altogether in the right; and this made her angrier than ever. She therefore preserved a sullen silence.

Boso said savagely, "They put on airs because they think Bambi will protect them."

"You will not mention your leader's name like that," Faline said sternly.

Rolla turned to face her one-time friend. "Faline," she said quietly, "it seems to me that Boso said nothing improper about Bambi. He said that *you* would not behave as you do if it were not for Bambi's position. And I'm afraid he's right. I'll be glad to be judged by Bambi at any time."

"Children," Faline commanded stiffly, "I see we've made a mistake in associating with these people. Let us go. There's no need to spoil our beautiful day."

With that she turned and galloped off. Shortly Geno and, more slowly, Gurri followed her.

Chapter Twenty-Five

HE SUCCEEDING DAY DAWNED
bright and fine, Faline and her children
returned to the meadow. No one else was
there. Rolla, Lana and Boso did not appear.
To Gurri the place seemed particularly empty; emptier, somehow, in the flooding sunshine than it would
have been on a day of gloom.

Pricked still by a conscience that she tried to stifle,
Faline asked her daughter what bothered her.

"Nothing," Gurri replied. "What should be bothering me?"

"I can see you're not happy," Faline insisted.

Gurri did not wish to answer, but she could not help it.

"I'm sorry about Aunt Rolla and the children," she admitted. "I feel that we haven't been fair to them."

"That's a very disloyal way to talk," Faline replied with annoyance in her voice.

"I'm sorry, Mother, but that's how I feel. I don't like to lose such old friends without a good reason."

"A good reason!" Faline trembled with anger. "You don't call it a good reason to . . ."

Gurri interrupted her.

"Very well, Mother, I'm sorry. Let me say simply that I'm sorry to lose good friends for *any* reason."

"Friends are easy to find," Faline snapped untruthfully.

She had hardly spoken when Geno noticed two young roe-bucks entering the meadow.

"Look," he said. "Strangers."

Faline followed the direction of his glance.

"Perhaps here are some new friends," she suggested.

Geno hurried to meet them.

"Hello!" he said.

The new arrivals regarded him rather sheepishly, but they finally greeted him.

"What are your names?" asked Geno.

"This is Nello," one of them replied, "and I am Membo."

He spoke with a sort of nervous desperation. The one named Nello was more grave.

"I am Geno, the son of Bambi," Geno told them, "and this is my sister, Gurri."

"Greetings, Gurri," the young bucks said. "We have heard of both of you."

"You have?" Geno exclaimed.

"Naturally we know of the son of Bambi," Nello said soberly, "and also of the daughter of Faline."

"What beautiful manners you have," remarked Gurri frankly.

The young bucks said nothing. Geno, looking at

them with interest, noticed the bumps on their heads that foretold their maturity to come. He thought, "My head looks like that."

Gurri said, "What are you doing here? We have never seen you before."

"We came because we were unhappy," Membo said.

Gurri could not help noticing that as he stood, with his weight lightly placed on one hind leg, he trembled violently.

"You seem very nervous, Membo," she said.

He had difficulty in answering her. "I—I'm s-sorry," he stammered.

"You must excuse him," Nello hurried to say. "He had a very bad experience during the terror when He came to kill."

"What was it?" Geno asked eagerly.

"Our mother was killed," Nello said reluctantly.

"Oh, I'm sorry!" cried Gurri. "Is that why you are alone?"

"Yes," replied Membo simply.

"Then you must meet our mother," decided Gurri.

She called Faline and introduced them to her. Faline was very gracious.

"You must play with Gurri and Geno," she said. "It doesn't do to mope, even after such a sad thing as that."

"Th-thank you!" said Membo.

Faline seemed to be lost in thought.

"I wonder," she said at last, "I wonder if you would like to stay with us."

"Stay with you?" said Membo wonderingly.

Faline felt that if she was very kind to these two orphans she would not have to reproach herself any longer for her injustice to Rolla.

"Yes," she replied. "I've often thought that when Geno began to grow up it would be nice for him to have male companions of his own age."

"You mean—stay with you forever?" Even the restrained Nello showed excitement.

"Oh, Madame Faline!" cried Membo.

"You must call me Mother if you decide to stay."

The brothers were deeply moved. They stammered their incoherent thanks, but Faline shrugged them away.

"Now you will have good friends," she said to Gurri.

"Better than friends!" Geno exclaimed excitedly.

"You are all t-too kind!" said Membo.

"Let's play!" Geno suggested.

The others agreed thankfully.

From then on, Geno was a leader to them. They felt that upon him descended the splendid mantle of Bambi, and while they were not subservient, they made him understand that they appreciated this distinction. Even though there was no difference in their ages, they treated him as an elder brother.

In the interest and pleasure of this new relationship, even Gurri hardly spared a thought for Lana and Boso. The two families seldom encountered each other; and when they did they behaved like strangers.

The brothers repeated again and again how happy they were.

"It makes us realize how incomplete life was for us before we were lucky enough to meet you," they told Faline.

As for Faline, if there had ever been any selfish

motive behind her adoption of the two young deer, it quickly passed. She came to be almost as fond of these newcomers to her family circle as she was of her own two children and tried at all times to show her equal affection for them.

The days passed happily. During their play, Membo surpassed them all in speed. When he ran, no one else could keep up with him; not even Geno who had hitherto been counted the fastest of the younger deer in the forest.

One day, when the five of them returned to their sleeping place, Gurri spoke of this to Nello.

"He has very strong hind legs," Nello said, "and, of course, his nervousness makes him faster."

"I think he is getting less nervous," Gurri remarked.

"I believe you are right, and that is to be expected under the circumstances."

"There's that squirrel," Geno broke in, "and he seems to have found his stores."

"I have found *some* stores," the squirrel corrected him. "I don't know whether they're mine or not."

"Squirrel," Gurri said accusingly, "I'm afraid you're a thief."

The squirrel almost choked on the nut he was eating.

"Well, of all the impudence!" he gasped.

"If you're taking someone else's savings, you're a thief," stated Gurri firmly.

"What nonsense!" squeaked the squirrel, his tail a bushy exclamation point. "What utter nonsense!"

His cheeks were puffed out both with indignation and the nuts he had stuffed in his pouches.

"Well, what else can you call yourself?" demanded Gurri with mock severity.

The squirrel's nose trembled. "I believe in the brotherhood of squirrels," he said loftily.

"Perhaps you should explain the brotherhood which entitles you to gobble up someone else's property," persisted Gurri.

"There is no such thing as property," the squirrel announced grandly. "Everything belongs to everybody."

"You're just a cuckoo with fur," Gurri said impudently.

"Why, really, you get worse every minute!" spluttered

the squirrel. "Let me tell you, young lady, I'm *old* enough to be your father, even if I'm not *big* enough, and that entitles me to a certain amount of respect. All the squirrels work hard when fall comes, gathering nuts and hiding them and forgetting where they put them."

"I told you you should learn to remember."

"Fiddlesticks! If you ask me, there's too much remembering going on. Suppose I did remember where I hid the nuts I gathered. If I saw someone else helping himself, I'd be angry and want to fight. What good would that do?"

Gurri was unable to find an answer to this argument, so the squirrel went on thoughtfully:

"Moreover, some other squirrel might have gathered better nuts than I had, and so I'd rather find his anyway."

"They might be worse, too," suggested Geno.

"That's not the way to look at it," declared the squirrel obstinately. "If you go around thinking you're being cheated, life becomes very unpleasant."

"That's true enough," admitted Gurri.

"Of course it's true. You're not going to call me a liar, too, I hope."

"But suppose," Nello interposed, "that some squirrel didn't gather any nuts at all? Would you be willing to let him steal the fruits of your labor?"

"You confuse the issue," announced the squirrel. "Nuts aren't fruit and never will be. The suggestion isn't true anyway. All squirrels gather nuts in autumn."

"But just suppose one didn't," insisted Nello.

"In that case," the squirrel said, "he'd be welcome to eat his fill. It would cost more time and effort to see that everybody gathered nuts than it would to support a lazy one like that."

Very calmly he cracked another nut. The roe-deer stretched themselves for sleep. The squirrel's mind was as active as his muscles. They needed time to think up proper answers to refute him.

Chapter Twenty-Six

SPRING HAD REALLY COME TO THE forest. The chestnuts were laden with sticky buds. The oak wore a lacy coat of green. The forest paths, the open glades and the meadow were misted with young grass and darkly patched with purple violets.

Already the swallow was darting ceaselessly around. The woodpecker's drill drummed against the trees. An early butterfly or two drifted on the wind, and bees went once more about their business.

The scent of growth, the sound of busy life were in the air. The breeze that blew was soft. It whispered to the daffodils who nodded back. Every day the concert of the birds swelled sweetly.

Gurri remembered the lark and spoke of it, of its heartwarming song, its modest mien and circumstances.

Membo said eagerly, "I should like to hear it sing."

Gurri shook her head. "It lives in the fields where He is always present. It's a dangerous song for us to hear."

The roe-deer lost their winter coats and put on brilliant summer red. Geno's crown grew in two horns each the size and thickness of a finger. These horns still kept a mosslike covering, but he was inordinately proud of them, looking at himself constantly in the mirror of the pool to discover if they had grown.

Membo and Nello also had their budding crowns, but theirs were not so far advanced as Geno's. This gave them additional cause to regard him as their chief.

The sapling took the tall oak's advice and grew with new vigor. Little by little it filled the space left it by the fallen branch. Silently but mightily it strove to achieve its purpose before the oak's leaves should become thick enough to reduce the rays of light that reached it.

The roe-deer, on the way to their meadow, ate the lower buds from tree and bush, rejoicing in their juiciness. Then they would run across the meadow, dodging and chasing one another, twisting, turning, bucking, stopping abruptly on stiffened legs, while the grass hissed silkily behind them.

Faline watched them fondly. All of them were handsome, agile, gay. Membo was much less nervous. Geno grew daily more like his father—in looks and in character.

Bambi did not visit them. His crown was slow in coming. He thought of them often, especially of Geno; but without his crown he felt he could not leave his retreat.

Most of the bucks roamed the forest paths again, their antlers fully grown, but still shrouded in their mossy covers. Soon they would strip these coverings away, leaving the naked points bright and shining.

The Kings, too, began to appear, still to the great dismay of Faline, although she made a brave effort to control her nervousness. She even spent time trying to persuade Membo and Nello of the beauty of the Kings and of their close relationship to the roe-deer. Nello and Membo were not so easily impressed with the soundness of these arguments, however, and their loud "ba-ohs" whenever the Kings appeared rang throughout the forest.

Gurri told her adopted brothers of the encounter she had witnessed between the rival Kings in the clearing.

"My goodness!" Membo exclaimed. "I certainly don't want to have anything to do with creatures who are as fierce as that!"

"But later in the year they were very gentle," Gurri mused.

"I wonder why," said Geno.

Finally Bambi came to see them.

His antlers had grown to their full dimensions. He had rubbed the covering skin from them on the stout trees of the forest and now, stained by the sap of the trees he had injured in stripping them, they gleamed bright as dark ivory.

Membo and Nello were awed at his appearance, but

they conducted themselves well, standing straight and still, awaiting his notice. He was in an affable mood, glad to be united with his family again, glad that he no longer had to lurk hidden from his kind in the recesses of his cave.

"Well," he said, after greeting his mate and children, "whom have we here?"

"This is Membo and this Nello," Faline informed him.

He saluted them courteously.

"They are my new children," Faline said.

"So-ho!" Bambi fixed them with his dark and brilliant eyes. "Your new children, are they! Well, this is rather a surprise."

Membo and Nello shifted uneasily.

"Who may your father be?" Bambi inquired.

"He's dead, sir," they replied. "He was slain by the thunder-stick."

"I have adopted them," Faline went on. "They have neither father nor mother."

"I see. Well, let me look at them."

Membo and Nello walked sheepishly before him.

"Nice lads," Bambi said at last. "They move well. They hold their heads high. How do they get on with our friends? With Lana and Boso, for instance?"

Silence fell upon them all. None of them knew how to answer.

"Well?" Bambi urged impatiently. "Are you all dumb?"

"We don't see them any more," Geno said at last.

"You don't see them! And why not?"

Faline told of Rolla's escape from the wolf-dog and Geno's subsequent peril.

Bambi listened gravely.

"And now," he summed up when she had finished, "Boso in particular feels that you have used his mother ill."

"Yes," Faline agreed. "Moreover, he accused me of shielding myself behind you, of taking advantage of your position to make life miserable for Rolla."

"He shouldn't have said that even if he believed it," Bambi decided. He thought for a while. "How is Rolla's leg?"

"I think it's all right. She limps only slightly."

"I see."

Again there was silence.

All of them felt uneasy, and when Bambi spoke again, it was almost as if they were startled by some stranger.

"Gurri," Bambi said, "will you allow me to speak with your mother and Geno alone for a moment?"

Gurri immediately led Membo and Nello away.

"Faline," Bambi continued, "Rolla undertook to be judged by me. This, then, I have to say: First, I think you have behaved wrongly. You can blame no one for the blindness of despair. You should try to patch up this difference with Rolla without delay. Second, it would have been more admirable for Geno to understand and make allowances for Boso. We are, rightly or wrongly, the first family among the roe-deer. If we cannot understand and forgive, we are not worthy of our station."

Faline hung her head. Bambi's voice put into clear words what her conscience had for a long time been whispering to her. She felt ashamed.

Geno said, "But, Father . . ."

"I see no necessity for argument, son. You are getting

your crown. If you cannot think and act like a grownup, you do not deserve it."

Faline cried impulsively, "You are right, of course. I have known it all along."

"Of course you have." Bambi nuzzled her affectionately. "Now let's take another look at these new children of ours."

Gurri returned with the two brothers. Faline understood the meaning of Bambi's possessive "ours" and was happy, both for herself and for her adopted sons.

"So," Bambi said to them, "you have been adopted by Faline. I am afraid there is nothing for it, then, except for me to adopt you too. Do you call her Mother?"

"Yes, sir," murmured Nello.

"Then you'll have to call me Father whether you like it or not. You see, I nearly always do what your mother wants me to."

"Oh, sir . . ." stammered Membo.

"Oh, what?" Bambi demanded with assumed fierceness.

"Oh . . ." Poor Membo could hardly get the word out. "Oh—F-father . . . !"

"That's it. It's a very easy word."

"But what a deal it means when it is said to Bambi," said Nello proudly.

"A very pretty speech, my boy. Now, I want all three of you to come with me."

Without a word Geno and the brothers followed him to a stout, low-branching shrub.

"Now, strip the covering from your antlers," he ordered Geno.

Clumsily Geno tried to obey, but his efforts were without much success. Patiently, Bambi taught him. Finally, Geno found the right way.

"There," Bambi exclaimed when the tiny horns shone clean as a fox's tooth, "we make progress. Now, Nello and Membo, when your crowns have grown as big as Geno's is now, act in the same way. Do not keep your antlers covered a moment longer than you need to.

"Your growing antlers," Bambi continued, "are proof of your intimate place in the forest, for of all the things that live and grow only the trees and the deer shed their foliage each year and replace it more strongly, more

magnificently, in the spring. Each year the trees grow larger and put on more leaves. And so you too increase in size and wear a larger, stronger crown."

"It is so," marveled Geno.

"Remember it," Bambi counseled them. "Be glad that you, and you only, are allied to the mighty oak and the spreading maple. Now I must go. I welcome you, Membo and Nello, to our family. Let us all strive to be worthy of each other. Goodbye."

They watched him dart through the sunshine and the shadow, his great muscles rippling, his antlers proud and gleaming.

"He is wonderful!" Nello murmured at last.

"Of course he is," Geno said with pride, "and we are his sons."

Aglow with their new maturity they returned to Faline and Gurri.

The oriole glittered as he flew from tree to tree crying his everlasting praise:

"I'm so happy!"

Chapter Twenty-Seven

RESTLESSNESS BEGAN TO STIR IN Geno like those hidden currents of a stream which, unseen though they may be, still bear insistently toward their goal.

He began to leave his mother's side, to undertake long explorations either in company with Nello and his brother, or, more often, alone.

He drew great excitement from these solitary wanderings, seeming to discover each tree and bush and plant, each herb and blade of grass, anew.

He visited his friends, discussing the affairs and events of the forest, feeling that now he played a real and personal part in them.

He made new friends, introducing himself to other roe-deer, young bucks generally more mature than he who, nevertheless, because he was the son of Bambi, treated him with much respect.

The nests built with so much labor when spring was new were now occupied by nesting birds. Geno visited these also, observing their habits, their troubles and their joys.

He saw the cock pheasants hustle their hens from their nests when twilight fell, urging them to take some exercise and get some food. He listened to the hens during their span of freedom as they gossiped together of their hopes and fears.

When the marauding crows and magpies came to rob the nests, he suffered with the hens who strove to drive them off. Yet even while he condemned the cruelty of these invaders, he could not help but admire the dexterity and cunning with which their forays were conducted.

He spoke of this to the screech-owl when he discovered him sitting sleepily on a branch. The screech-owl shrugged.

"The best line of defense," he muttered, "is attack. That is the first law of strategy."

"Perhaps so," admitted Geno, "but if the mother birds spent their time attacking, who would hatch out their broods?"

"I have no idea," said the screech-owl and promptly lapsed into slumber.

Geno turned away just as Lana emerged from behind a near-by bramble. Without thinking he greeted her.

She stopped at once.

"I thought you weren't speaking to us," she said.

Confronted with a direct accusation, Geno felt rather foolish.

"I?" he said, "I didn't think I had very much to do with it."

"Oh, I suppose you want to blame it all on Boso!"

Geno remembered Bambi's words of counsel. "No. Oh no, I don't want to blame anyone."

"Then why do you behave like such a boor?"

"Do you think me discourteous?"

"I don't think of you at all!" Lana lifted her head very high and stared at Geno hard and haughtily.

It was impossible for Geno to think of any retort to this bald statement, so he just stared back at her. If she hadn't such a bad temper, he thought, she would be quite good-looking. Her new red coat was sleek and smooth.

"Where are you going?" she demanded when she thought the silence had lasted long enough.

"Nowhere. I'm just wandering around."

"You do waste your time, don't you?"

"How can you waste time? You have only so much to use, and no matter what you do, it still passes."

"Why don't you come to see us?"

"I thought I wouldn't be welcome."

"I sometimes think males shouldn't think. They need all their heads for growing antlers." She stopped. "Yours are quite long, aren't they?"

Her voice was suddenly so soft that Geno was startled.

"Long enough, I guess," he muttered.

"How is Gurri?"

"Very well."

"You have some new brothers, too."

"Yes."

"I saw them. They are very handsome."

"I'm glad you think so."

"But not," again that softness invaded her voice, "not so handsome as you, Geno."

Geno felt his chest expand. "I'm glad you think so, Lana."

"I sometimes think you're the handsomest one in the forest."

"Lana!"

"Except of course for Boso," she concluded in a dreamy voice.

"Boso!" His voice flamed with scorn. "Why let me tell you . . ."

"Tell her what?"

Geno spun around. Unheard, Boso had advanced and now stood to one side of him. The young bucks faced each other.

"Tell her—*what*?" repeated Boso.

"Nothing," said Geno.

"Very well. Then we'll fight."

"Fight? What for?"

"Because I don't like your looks. That's reason enough."

Boso lowered his head and pawed the ground with his front hoof.

Geno said, "But I don't want to fight."

"I'm coming!" roared Boso, and charged.

Geno spun on his hind hoofs and fled. The screech-owl wakened.

"He who fights and runs away," he said, "may live to fight another day."

"Coward!" Boso yelled after the flying Geno.

Lana said furiously, "Leave him alone, will you! You're just a bully."

The screech-owl intoned, "Happy is the man whose cause is just, but happier he who gets his blow in fust!"

"That's an awful rhyme," stormed Lana.

"I didn't make it up," replied the screech-owl, and closed his eyes again.

Back in the clearing, Geno told his mother and Gurri what had happened.

"But, Geno," Gurri remonstrated, "why did you run away? You're not a coward, are you?"

"I don't know why I ran away. All I know is I didn't want to fight Boso."

"Was it Boso you didn't want to fight, or was it Lana's brother?" queried Faline softly.

"I can't see any difference," Geno muttered.

All the same, he spent considerable time asking himself why he had run away. Could it be that he was a coward? It seemed terrible to imagine that the son of Bambi could be anything but brave.

Chapter Twenty-Eight

FROM THEN ON, BOSO TRIED TO throw himself in Geno's path. His instinct was to increase the advantage he had gained over Geno, either by defeating him in battle or by causing him to seek refuge again in flight.

He had not bargained on meeting his adversary in the company of his two newly acquired brothers, but when this happened he decided not to back down until he had exchanged a satisfactory number of insults with them. He was by this time so convinced of Geno's cowardice and of his own outstanding courage that nothing could daunt him.

Membo was the first to see Boso moving through the undergrowth toward them.

"G-geno," he cried, his stammering made worse by excitement, "B-boso is c-coming."

Geno stopped dead.

"Oh," he said uncertainly.

"Don't worry," Nello urged him. "We are with you."

"I'm not worrying," asserted Geno.

Boso came within hailing distance.

"So," he said tauntingly, "you brought a few friends along today, eh? Well, do you think the three of you can stand still and take what's coming to you?"

"S-s-see h-h-h-," began Membo; but before he could get the words out, Geno said mildly:

"Boso, I don't want to fight you."

"Oh, you don't. Well, I have a different idea."

"Geno," Nello whispered, "I'm afraid there's no way out. You'll have to teach this fellow a lesson."

Geno stared down at the ground.

"No," he said stubbornly, "I don't want to fight."

With that determined statement, he turned and trotted away. Membo and Nello watched his retreat with astonishment.

"Huh!" Boso sneered. "Maybe I'd better send the hare to do my fighting. It seems I'm too big for your friend."

"You're not too big for me," Nello quietly advised him, "and you'd better be careful."

"It's easy for you to talk," Boso said. "There are two of you. Anyhow, I've no quarrel with either of you. My quarrel is with Geno. If he's too cowardly to fight, that's all there is to it."

In fairness, Nello could find nothing wrong with this argument. He signaled to Membo and the two of them walked forlornly after Geno.

That evening Geno was aware of the distrust in the hearts of all about him. Even Faline was subdued. The roe-deer were still sleeping at night, and Membo and Nello only waited for the females to go off to sleep before they demanded an explanation from their adopted brother.

"It just doesn't make sense," they argued. "You're at least as big and as strong as Boso."

"I'm sorry," Geno said.

"But listen," Nello, who usually said little, found speech rushing to him: "this has gone beyond the personal question of whether you will or will not fight Boso. Your reputation throughout the forest is at stake. Perhaps . . ." he hesitated . . ."perhaps even Bambi's!"

"What difference would a fight between Boso and me make to my father's reputation?" queried Geno scornfully.

"It might be quite important. None of us can afford to take the risk of damaging it."

Gurri said softly, "I'm sure Geno will work his problem out."

The brothers were surprised to hear Gurri's voice. They had believed her asleep. Geno said nothing, but he was grateful for her intervention.

Next morning he got up early, but not earlier than Gurri.

"I'd like to walk with you today," she said.

"By all means."

"Where are you going?"

"Oh, just around. Nowhere in particular."

"That's what I feel like. A lazy day."

"Let's go, then."

They drifted slowly along, admiring the foliage of the trees, the flowers that bloomed on the sunny side of grassy banks. Geno told his sister what his father had said about the likeness that existed between the trees and the deer.

"What a splendid idea!" Gurri said enthusiastically.

"I thought so," Geno concurred. "I wish we could see more of Father."

"You will, soon," Gurri assured him.

They came to the meadow and the pool. Metal-colored dragon-flies shuttled back and forth, or spread their shimmering wings in rest upon a broad dock leaf. Frogs sprang from the banks as they passed, diving into the water and swimming vigorously below the surface until they reached the other side. Both Geno and Gurri drank of the water before they continued on their way.

They watched a nest of ants purposeful about their business, and stood quietly while a spider spun its intricate, deceiving web.

They poked black noses into bushes where nesting birds sat quietly on their eggs: thrushes, tomtits, sparrows, robins, all concerned with the intimate cares of preparing for the baby birds.

Once Geno glanced up into a half-dead elm. Two huge black birds sat on a broken bough. He had a sudden feeling that he knew them. He was right.

One of them said, "It's young never-say-die."

"So it is. He looks well, doesn't he?"

"How do you do?" said Geno. "This is my sister."

"Pleased to meet you," said the second crow.

"You look well, too," Geno told them.

"I should think so," the first one said. "Would you like to know what we've eaten since yesterday?"

Gurri shuddered. "No thank you."

"Just as you say. But talking of food reminds me. I know where there's a nice little snack to be picked up." He whispered hoarsely to his companion. The two of them flapped off their supporting bough. "Goodbye. We'll see you again, perhaps!"

"Birds and He are alike in some ways," Gurri murmured.

"What do you mean?"

"They seem to be capable of so much harm and so much good. I wish I could understand why He both feeds us and kills us. I think I should then have the answer to a lot of things that puzzle me."

Without noticing where they were going, they had wandered back to their clearing. Neither Faline nor the brothers were there. It lay peaceful and empty under the sun, seeming to stretch before their thoughtful eyes.

Gurri said abruptly: "There's Perri. She seems to be in a terrible hurry."

They watched the squirrel swing nimbly from tree to tree until she had arrived at her private branch on the oak.

"What's the matter?" Gurri asked.

"There's trouble on the way again," she said excitedly. "I just heard the news. There's a young fox in the district."

"A young fox! Does the hare know?"

"I'll give him the bad news as soon as I see him. Much worse from my point of view is the marten."

"Is there a marten, too?"

"Yes. A big creature. If I could only understand what good martens are in the scheme of things!"

"I was just saying much the same thing about Him."

"Well, Gurri, He kills martens sometimes. Really, when I come to think of it, I have little to grumble at in Him."

"I never thought of that before." Gurri looked puzzled. "When you consider the matter, there are only a few of us who have to be frightened of Him."

"Whereas martens do no good to anything."

"I guess we're getting to be too big for either the fox or the marten to do us much harm."

"You're lucky," grumbled Perri. "If I were only as big as you, now, I'd give the marten what for—I give you my word."

"You haven't seen Lana or Boso around, I suppose," Geno asked casually.

"Boso, no, but Lana was not so far from here a little while back. I saw her myself."

"Thank you." Geno was just turning away, when Perri called him closer.

"Listen, Geno," she whispered hurriedly, "of course it's none of my business, but if it's Lana who is holding you back from whipping Boso, forget it. I've lived longer than you, my boy, and she won't hold it against you for long."

"There's my father, too," Geno objected. "He wanted me to make it up with Boso."

"Well, I'll tell you about that too. A fellow like Boso must have his fight before he can get around to thinking about making peace. And that's another funny thing you'll learn as you get older. You can't just have a state of peace. You've got to have war first and then *make* peace."

"I see," said Geno. "Well, thank you for your advice. I think I'll be getting along."

At this moment there was a rustle behind the elder bush and a young buck ran up to them. He was older than Geno, if not fully mature. His name was Até, and Geno had met him during his lonely wanderings through the woodlands.

"Hello, Geno," he said, "it's nice to see you."

Gurri, who had wandered away to give Perri a chance to talk in private with Geno, looked up. Até noticed her at once.

"Who's that?" he asked.

"That's my sister. Gurri," called Geno, "I'd like to have you meet Até, a friend of mine."

Gurri came over and the two met.

"You are very lovely, Gurri," Até murmured, his eyes flashing.

"Really?" Gurri replied coldly. "I'm glad you think so.

Até was not in the least abashed.

"How could I think otherwise?" he asked.

"Do you know my brother well?" Gurri inquired. After the introduction Geno had gone on ahead. He seemed to be looking for something.

"We've met several times. We are good friends."

"Then perhaps you would tell me," Gurri hesitated,

"what you think of—his running away from Boso?"

"Oh, that!" Até said dramatically. "A deer does not wish to attack his loved one's brother."

"You mean, Geno loves Lana! But he's too young!"

"How can one be too young for love?" Até asked.

"But *is* he really in love?"

"I don't know. But it seems altogether possible."

"Why" said Gurri. "there *is* Lana, and Geno is with her."

Até turned to see Geno and Lana in earnest conversation.

"Well," he said with a sudden change of tone, "I think this is it!"

"This is what?"

"Well, if Boso comes along now he's likely to run into trouble!"

Lana and Geno disappeared into the shadows of the trees. Gurri and Até followed.

Suddenly Bambi appeared in front of them.

"Father!" began Gurri; but he quieted her.

"Not a sound," he said, "I want to see what happens."

"You know?" Gurri inquired.

"Of course I know."

He melted into the underbrush. Gurri and a more respectful Até followed in Geno's path.

They came up with Geno and Lana in a clearing. Lana looked up when she heard their hoofbeats.

"Oh, Gurri," she cried, "It's *nice* seeing you!"

"I'm glad to see you," Gurri replied sincerely.

"I was just going. Perhaps you'd like to walk with me."

"I'd like it very much."

"Perhaps I could escort you both," suggested Até.

All of them were surprised to hear Perri's voice again directly above them.

"I followed you," she said, "to keep a lookout. Boso's coming."

"Oh dear, perhaps you'd better stay then, Gurri," said Lana.

"Not at all. On your way, all of you," commanded Geno.

Até's eyes sparkled.

"Come on," he said. He led them away.

Geno heard Boso's careless advance a long way off.

He dashed into the clearing, looking as fierce as he could.

"Were you talking to my sister?" he demanded.

"I was, as a matter of fact."

"I forbid it, do you hear? I won't allow it."

"I'm afraid it has nothing to do with you."

"Oh, it hasn't, eh! You'd better get ready to run again. There are ways of making you do things."

"I'd like to learn them."

Boso wasted no more time, but rushed into a charge. Geno waited until Boso was almost on him and stepped lightly to one side. His own impetus carried Boso head foremost into a thick and thorny bramble. He emerged fuming.

"So you still can't stand up and face me. What do you think this is, a dance?"

"It looked rather like a mole at work. Except that moles have more sense than to bore holes in thornbushes."

"All right, smarty. Look out for yourself."

Boso charged again; but this time Geno did not

move. He remained planted like a rock, his four legs extended like the piers of an arch. Boso bounced off him as a chestnut bounces when it hits the ground.

"You'll catch a dreadful headache that way," murmured Geno.

"I'll kill you!" raged Boso. "I'll break you in pieces."

He charged and, turning, charged again. Geno met his onrushes calmly. Head to head they strove together as the Kings had done, except that neither Geno nor Boso had the great entangling antlers to make their efforts deadly.

Boso broke free and charged once more. This time Geno ran to meet him. They met with a terrific shock. Boso reeled. Pouncing on his advantage, Geno smashed into Boso's flank. Boso gave ground and again Geno charged. The unfortunate Boso almost left the ground. He shot sideways and landed on his back.

Geno retired.

For a time there was no sound save the hoarse breathing of the fighters. Then Boso scrambled dizzily to his feet.

"Boso," Geno said, "we've had our fight. Now let's be friends."

Boso did not reply.

Geno went on, "I think you've been very badly treated by all of us, and I'm sorry. Can't things be as they were?"

The moment to make peace had come, but Boso did not take advantage of it. With his head lowered, he staggered blindly away.

Até, Gurri and Lana came out from the undergrowth.

"You watched," Geno accused them.

"And a very good fight it was," said Até.

Lana was trembling.

"You shouldn't have done that," Geno said quietly. "Lana, I'm sorry,"

"Don't come near me," Lana cried. "Até, take me home at once, please."

Gurri softly nuzzled her brother.

"Don't worry, Geno," she said. "I'm sure things will come out all right."

"I hoped no one would see," he mumbled. "I didn't want it talked about."

"You know the forest is always full of eyes," said Gurri. "You can't expect to keep a thing like this secret."

Slowly Geno followed her back to the clearing.

Chapter Twenty-Nine

FALINE KNEW OF GENO'S ADVENTURE
before he and Gurri arrived at the clearing.
Bambi had hurried to tell her. Both Faline and
Bambi congratulated themselves on Geno's
prowess.

"It is not so much the fact that he fought," mused
Bambi, "as that he restrained himself for so long. He
tried to obey me in every way he knew and show his
friendship for Boso."

"Of course he did," agreed Faline, smiling silently.

She felt that there was more to Geno's restraint than even the wise Bambi suspected; but she kept her opinion to herself.

"I am disappointed in one thing," Bambi confessed. "I admit I thought that a fight between Geno and Boso would lead to their making up. But it seems to have done just the opposite."

"I'm sure things will come out all right," murmured Faline, unconsciously echoing the words her daughter was speaking in another part of the forest.

"Lana was most upset."

"She'll get over it."

"I suspect you're right."

Bambi rubbed his antlers thoughtfully against the trunk of a tree.

"I suppose I must be going, but I'll see you again soon."

"I shall look forward to it," Faline assured him.

She watched him pick his rapid, skillful way among the trees, her heart light within her.

Nello and Membo also heard the news from the hare.

"Perri told me," the hare explained. "Bless my soul and whiskers, it was a mighty victory. You know, I'm much against violence, but Geno actually knocked him down."

The hare boxed with his little forepaws.

Membo grinned.

"I'll b-bet you were quite a fellow yourself once."

The hare looked startled.

"Me? Oh, dear no! As a runner, now, I was in a class by myself. Quite a lad, I was, I assure you. I ran a very famous race with a tortoise once."

"But you didn't win that."

"No, it's true I didn't win. . . ." The hare ended his recollections abruptly. "Oh, dear me," he said with a shiver, "I almost forgot the bad news Perri brought me about the fox. It just goes to show you mustn't let yourself be carried away. Excuse me, I think I'd better go into hiding. It's been very nice seeing you."

Membo and Nello turned to leave.

"Be sure to offer Geno my sincere congratulations," the hare called after them; but when they turned to tell him they would, he had disappeared.

Geno, in fact, was overwhelmed with congratulations. To escape them and the constant requests by different members of the forest society to repeat his tale of conquest, he took to wandering by himself again.

Always during these trips he at some time felt the need of a drink of water.

One day he went farther afield than usual and retraced his steps over the ground he had covered during his frantic flight from the wolf-dog. Eventually, just when he was becoming unbearably thirsty and was scolding himself for not having quenched his thirst at the pool where the willow-tree grew, he came to the stream which, when he had last seen it, had been reduced by frost to a trickle of its usual self.

Now it ran merrily, hurling itself in joyous abandon over mossy rocks, dashing in tiny cataracts over ledges shaded by tall ferns and finally broadening into a peaceful pool.

A heron stood there, still balancing himself on one lanky leg, absent-mindedly reaching into the water once in a while to swallow some unlucky frog.

"Why, heron," Geno said, "I didn't know you'd left the pool in our meadow."

"I haven't," the heron replied with harsh finality.

"Well, I mean—" Geno did not wish to appear to contradict— "you're hardly there now, are you?"

"I just came here for a change. Any idiot could tell that," snapped the heron.

Geno thought the heron was rude. He looked around. A couple of full-grown ducks were teaching a squadron of ducklings to swim with a great deal of squawking and flourishing of stubby tails.

"Wa-ak, wa-ak! Wa-ak, wa-ak, wa-ak, wa-ak!" said one mother duck impatiently.

Three small, yellow ducklings executed a left-hand turn.

"Wa-ak, wa-ak, wa-ak—wa-a-a-a-a-k!" said the mother.

The ducklings swam lustily in single file. All except one, that is, who hurried nervously off in the opposite direction.

"Wa-ak, wa-a-ak!" snapped its mother.

The little duckling turned so sharply that it almost rolled over in the water and paddled protestingly after the others.

"E-eek!" it said. "E-eekeek!"

Its mother waggled her tail and snapped her bill a couple of times.

"Wa-ak, wa-ak!" she said abruptly.

The ducklings bustled toward the shore and struggled into cover.

The mother duck dove absent-mindedly and came up right under Geno's nose.

"Hello," Geno said.

The duck looked at him suspiciously with round black eyes. "Well?" she squawked impatiently.

The other mother duck who had been putting her fleet of young through much the same movements as her neighbor called out:

"Don't waste your time talking to him. We've a lot to do."

"I can take a minute for myself, can't I?"

"How many children have you got?" Geno inquired.

"Of what possible importance can that be?" asked the duck,

"It seems important," Geno said. "It would be to me."

"It might be to the fish," the heron interposed unexpectedly.

"To the fish!" Geno repeated, rather bewildered.

"Certainly. The more ducks, the fewer fish and vice versa."

"Oh, I see."

"You don't," remarked the heron coldly, "but you would if you were a fish."

"I suppose that's true," admitted Geno.

"Of course it's true." The heron changed legs and scooped a frog up in its beak in one and the same motion.

From the cover where the ducklings lay hidden rose an agitated chorus of "Eeks!" The mother duck spun around.

"Wa-ak, wa-ak!" she squawked urgently.

The little ducklings came tumbling into the water.

"You see what you almost did?" she quacked irritably to Geno as she hurried to meet them.

Geno did realize what he had almost done when the scent of the fox reached him. He stiffened nervously.

A young dog-fox came furtively out of cover. He had hardly grown his second coat and his brush was still thin and immature. He took no notice of Geno, but sidled to the water close to the spot where the heron was standing.

"Nice day," he said in an oily voice.

"Is it?" the heron replied indifferently.

The heron seemed to be quite blind to the fox, but when the fox sprang at him his movements were like lightning. His long beak shot out like a spear.

"You might have got my eye!" the fox said in an injured tone, as he fell back.

"Indeed," rasped the heron, "I'll be more careful next time."

This kind of casual, undeclared warfare amazed Geno; but apparently it was as vicious as any preceded by the proper roarings and stampings to which he was used.

The fox sprang again, and again the wicked bill thrust dangerously. This time the fox yelled with pain.

"I warned you I'd be more careful," said the heron.

The fox said nothing. He peered at his adversary out of one good eye.

"I'll be seeing you again," he threatened somberly.

"Only out of one eye," replied the heron.

Silently Geno and the heron watched the fox retire. The mother ducks with their broods came out of the reeds where they had hidden.

The heron said, "That fox will learn."

Geno walked back toward the forest, wrapped in thought. This constant proof of the struggle to survive was almost threatening.

"From the smallest insect up to Him," he thought, "no safety and no peace. Can He also be afraid of something?"

A voice spoke to him from a near-by hazel.

"You're a thoughtful fellow," the voice said.

Geno glanced upward. A finch sat on a branch. He was blowing his breast feathers out to make himself look more important, but under this camouflage the bird appeared to be ill-nourished.

"I try to be," Geno answered.

"Well, I'll show you something that will astound you. Look!"

Geno approached the nest which the bird indicated. Inside it sat a fledgling of such size that it completely filled its modest quarters.

"What do you think of that?" the finch inquired proudly. "Isn't that amazing?"

"I should say it is!" Geno agreed whole-heartedly.

"I'll bet there's not another finch like that in the forest. I'll bet there's not another finch like that anywhere!" The proud father hopped along the branch and peered at the young one. "My goodness," he said, "what a bird! Look at that throat, will you?"

The father staggered a little when he mentioned the throat and Geno was afraid he was going to fall right into it.

"Steady!" he cried.

The finch looked a little annoyed.

"I seem to have the staggers," he fretted. "I think it's working so hard to get enough food for this child. Great oaks and elder bushes, you never saw such an appetite!"

There was a flutter in the leaves above them. The finch's mate arrived, carrying a large piece of worm in her beak.

"Go on," she scolded the father when she had dropped it into the youngster's mouth. "Don't stand there gawping! Get some more!"

She rested on the branch watching her son. Muttering to himself, the father flew away.

"That bird's twice as large as both of you put together," Geno told her.

"Isn't he though!"

"Did you have others?" Geno inquired.

"Oh, yes, he was one of five, but the others sickened and died. I don't know why."

The mother looked rather crestfallen, but she soon cheered up.

"Well," she said, "he makes up for them in size, anyhow. He'll be the most important finch anywhere, if you ask me."

"You don't look too well yourself, Ma'am."

"Don't I? I guess it's the heat. Or the humidity, maybe."

"I think you work too hard for your son."

"Nonsense! How could I do that?" She whistled a little tune deep in her throat.

The young bird's beak gaped. He made an angry sound.

"All right," she said, "your father will be back in a minute, and then I'll see what I can find."

The father finch returned with a huge grub.

"You'll upset his little stomach with that rich food," the mother bird scolded him. "For goodness' sake, haven't you any sense?"

"No, my love—I mean, yes, my love!" He watched the grub slide down the gaping throat. "Upset that one?" he added. "I don't believe you could upset him if you fed him hornets!"

"Don't you ever eat yourselves?" Geno asked.

"Oh, once in a while. We're too busy to think much about it." The mother took a last look at her charge before she flew after more food.

"Well, take care of yourselves," Geno advised as he left. "You're important, too, don't forget."

He had not gone very far before he met Até. Geno told him about the finches' amazing offspring.

"Oh," grinned Até, "that wasn't a finch! That was a cuckoo."

"A cuckoo!"

"Certainly."

"Then what was it doing in the finches' nest?"

"The cuckoo left it there when the finches weren't looking. She goes around in spring leaving her eggs in any nest she can and then, when they are hatched out by some other unsuspecting bird, she doesn't have the bore of rearing them."

"How perfectly dreadful!" Geno stopped dead in his tracks. "I'm going back to tell the finches at once."

Até stopped him. "It wouldn't do the slightest good," he said seriously. "They wouldn't believe you. It would make them very unhappy. When the young cuckoo leaves them, they'll soon forget."

Geno might have argued further, but he was startled by the sound of a shot.

"The thunder-stick!" he groaned. "My goodness, is the time of peace over?"

"It's very early for the thunder-stick," Até muttered, surprise subduing his usually clear tones.

A succession of shots crackled in the distance.

"Well, I guess there's no doubt about it," Até concluded resignedly. "We must go home carefully."

They took to cover. Every now and then the far-off roar of the thunder-stick was heard again.

Chapter Thirty

PERRI HASTENED DOWN HER TREE toward the roe-deer gathered in the clearing. Her fur was standing out quite straight with indignation.

"Never in all my life," she gasped. "Never in all my born days . . . !"

"What's the matter?" asked Nello.

"The thunder-stick!" Perri's emotion paralyzed her voice. "I—I—why, it went off at *me*!"

"At you?" exclaimed Gurri. "Why, I thought you said . . ."

"I know! I know!" Perri interrupted her. "I was wrong, that's all. I tell you, I don't know what things are coming to. You hold beliefs, you—you cling to certain basic principles and—pam! everything blows away around you."

"After me, the deluge," the screech-owl muttered.

Perri jerked around to face him. "What was that?"

"Nothing. I was merely commenting on the weather. Whom else is the thunder-stick attacking? Not owls, I hope."

"Some pigeons and a few magpies."

"How extraordinary!" Faline murmured.

A woodpecker flew down to join them. She was laughing wildly. "I've been shot at! Can you imagine that! Shot at! Me!"

"But you weren't hit?"

"No. But that's not the point. It's an outrage, that's what it is."

They fell to discussing this lightning war. Gurri

remembered the great horned owl's comment, made long before, about the thunder-stick:

"I've watched it very carefully and sometimes it goes off and nothing happens."

The chatter among the forest creatures ceased. Bambi had arrived. He greeted them quietly.

"I've heard something of what you've been saying," he said.

"Do you know anything about it?" Perri asked.

"Yes. The smaller animals and birds must be very careful. This killer is a young He. I can tell He's young because the skin He wears on His legs is short and there's no fur on His face. I suppose He's learning to kill. His thunder-stick is very small, too, not big enough to harm anything larger than a polecat. In fact, He has killed a polecat on the outskirts of the forest. But He doesn't aim the thunder-stick very well. If you are careful, none of you need come to harm."

Gurri thought, "Then the great horned owl was right. He does direct the thunder-stick."

Bambi continued, "The brown He has been teaching

Him, but the brown He is taking no part in the attack, and the young He is often left to His own devices."

Bambi was quite correct.

A boy of about fourteen was taking his first lessons with a gun. He was enthusiastic over his new sport and shot at everything he saw. He had beginner's luck, for after he had hit the polecat, he caught sight of the marten and wounded it so severely that it died.

The gamekeeper congratulated his pupil on this feat.

"Many a good pheasant will live the longer for that," he said.

Nevertheless, he determined to stop this shooting.

The boy's father was an important man in the district and it had been hard for the gamekeeper to refuse to teach his son the art of the gun and rifle; but it was bad for the deer to disturb them at this season of the year.

"You've had a lot of fun," he told the boy, "but you'll have to be patient for a few weeks longer before you can start in seriously. This is not the season."

The boy was not pleased at having his sport interrupted, but he was forced to agree.

Peace returned to the forest.

It was the calm before the storm.

After his quarrel with the heron the fox retired to his den to recover. His wound healed slowly.

Because it was difficult for him to hunt he grew thin from lack of food. Brooding over his condition—his pain, his hunger—his temper, naturally sour, turned savage. He came to hate all created things. A lust to kill rose in him.

When he finally recovered, One-Eye the fox became the terror of the district.

One-Eye ranged far abroad. He was not content to confine himself to the area near the stream. He found much better hunting in the part of the forest where the roe-deer lived.

Wherever he went, he left strewed behind him a trail of his victims' bones; their last flurries were clearly printed in the earth.

He grew big and strong. His coat took on a lustrous depth. His brush grew thick and long.

One-Eye was known and feared by all; all, that is, except certain of the deer and the heron.

The fox never forgot the heron. At the bottom of the hate that filled his heart and body was a seed from which it sprang. That seed was the memory of the heron.

Perhaps this hatred overflowed against all birds. Perhaps it was because of this that One-Eye became such a scourge to the pheasants.

The gamekeeper found skeleton after skeleton, some picked clean, some simply used for sport and left in tattered balls of blood and feathers. Stolidly he followed this trail of corpses. It led him far from the forest, across an open field, past the pool where the willow flourished greenly, over a sparkling stream where a litter of feathers was a memorial for some slain duck, into a tangled coppice of trees and bushes.

At his heels Hector trotted patiently. Over his

shoulder he carried not only his shotgun but a spade. In a deep thicket he discovered One-Eye's lair, a narrow hole hidden by creeping plants.

Swiftly he gathered brushwood which he thrust into the entrance to the den. Thoughtfully he packed his pipe and, with the match he used to light it, set the pyre to burning.

A column of smoke surged upward. Flames crackled merrily. But some inward curve in the hole kept the smoke and flame from entering.

The gamekeeper waited for the flames to die. He took his spade and attacked the sandy earth. Hector sat stiffly watching these activities, his eager eyes intent.

But nothing happened. Empty as an opened oyster-shell the lair lay bare. A narrow, backward-running tunnel told the story. One-Eye had not only a way in but also a way out.

The gamekeeper cursed but was not upset. He laid a snare or two in likely places and retraced his steps; but One-Eye left the skeletons of slaughtered hares and pheasants near the snares as though in mockery.

Naturally he did not return to his den. That was ruined as a home. He took to gipsying, sleeping in any suitable place. Every path and trail, every thicket and cave, were known to him, even Bambi's cave on the hillside.

He was bound for Bambi's cave at sun-up one morning when he crossed the clearing where Faline and her family slept. They were not there, but Perri was on the ground near the hazel bushes seeking some morsel with which to break her fast. Immediately One-Eye flattened down on his belly and crept toward the unsuspecting squirrel.

Like a puffball borne on a playful breeze Perri capered ahead of One-Eye, now darting a few steps forward, now rising upright while she searched the grass with eager, beady eyes. One-Eye slightly increased his pace. Two good springs and Perri would be his. One snap of that snarling mouth and another corpse would moulder with the others.

A voice said quietly, almost as though it were a matter for laughter:

"Quick, Perri! One-Eye's on your tail!"

One-Eye spun round with astonishment. Perri leaped to safety.

"So you're One-Eye," said Bambi.

The fox and the roe-deer faced each other. Bambi's head was held high, a beautiful mark for any throat-tearing killer; but One-Eye knew better.

"And you're Bambi," he replied.

"You have heard of me?" Bambi pretended surprise. "Do you allow any of your victims time for conversation? Aren't you afraid that some rabbit will attack you one of these days if you give him time to talk?"

One-Eye said nothing. His cunning brain was weighing chances, wondering if it would be possible, perhaps, to attack an animal this size successfully. Bambi read his thoughts.

"Don't hesitate! Spring! The heron didn't have as many prongs as I!"

"Don't be ridiculous," One-Eye said slyly. "I wouldn't dream of attacking you."

"I think perhaps you're telling the truth for once. I'm a little bigger and a little better protected than a

hare. Now I'll give you another invitation. Come to my cave sometime when I'm there. Believe me, I'll give you a welcome that will stay in your memory a long time."

"I come to your cave!" exclaimed One-Eye with a great show of astonishment.

"That's right. Sometime when I'm there."

"My dear Bambi," One-Eye said, "it's very kind of you, of course, but I swear I don't even know where your cave is."

"That's very strange," Bambi remarked, "it smells of you once in a while."

"Someone else, I assure you."

"No. You. Your scent is rather peculiar, you know."

One-Eye looked thoughtful.

"It couldn't be that place on the hillside which the dead tree hides."

"So! I see we understand each other."

"But I hadn't the remotest idea . . . !"

"Of course you hadn't! But now you know. I'll be waiting for you, if you live long enough!"

"If I live long enough!" The fox looked startled. "That's an unpleasant thing to say."

"You should know," said Bambi sternly, "that your kind doesn't flourish for long. You've an enemy more cunning than I and quicker than the heron."

"Who?" whispered One-Eye.

"The brown He."

The fox laughed. "Oh, I see. I was worried for a moment. Don't worry about me because of Him. I have proved myself more than a match for Him."

"Pride goeth before a fall," screeched a new voice.

Bambi glanced up. "Quite right, screech-owl," he agreed. "Others have tried to fight in a duel with Him. All of them are dead."

With that retort Bambi sprang into the bushes. One-Eye stood listening and thinking. The sneer faded from his face.

Chapter Thirty-One

OLDEN SUMMER DAYS SPED ON. Each morning the dew lay heavier in the hollows. Each evening the departing sun painted more colorful pictures in the western sky.

The noons were lazier, the scents that drifted in the air were heavy-sweet. Already now the hedgerows gleamed with cups of pinkly tinted roses, and leaning fence-posts bloomed with columbine. Wherever sunlight pierced the forest, midges swarmed and drowsy flies buzzed heavily.

"The time has come," said Bambi, "to sleep by day and take the forest paths when darkness falls. Be careful, now, for the thunder-stick will shortly start its business of destruction." He turned to Geno. "You understand, my son?"

Geno nodded simply. He understood that with those four simple words his father placed him in charge of the family; and so it was.

Faline ceased to lead and counsel. Now it was Geno who led the family forth at evening and brought them back with dawn's approach.

He took his duties seriously. Not a rustle disturbed the underbrush that he did not hear; not a scent moved in the air that he did not sample and understand.

Then, as Bambi had predicted, the thunder-stick was heard again.

The roe-deer had just lain down to sleep. It was a pearl-gray morning with a heavy mist above the ground that dampened the rays of the sun. The forest birds were sleepy, late with their song. Even the blackbird had done no more than clear his throat.

Nello and Membo had already closed their eyes. Geno and Gurri talked in whispers. Faline thought her private thoughts.

"We have seen less of One-Eye lately," Gurri said.

"Since he saw Father."

"Yes." Gurri shivered, although the morning was not cold. "I wish I could forget to be afraid of him."

"I'm sure you have no need for fear. You're not so small as you were when the brown He rescued you."

"I've told myself that. I'm like Mother when she sees the Kings, I suppose. I know that One-Eye will not harm me, and yet I am afraid."

"Listen!" Geno commanded.

They heard the heavy sound of the thunder-stick— once, twice.

Perri came hurtling through the trees. In misty weather or clear, she was about her business at the sun's first rising.

"One of your kind," she advised them. "A young buck."

Geno and Gurri were silent, grieving.

The noise of the reports had awakened Nello and Membo.

"Is it coming this way?" they queried anxiously.

"I don't think so." Perri worked her jaws nervously. "I've had a greater sympathy with your peril since I myself was a target for the thunder-stick."

"Then perhaps you'll use even more watchfulness on our behalf," said Geno shrewdly.

Perri was offended.

"I'm sure I've always tried to do my duty," she said.

"Of course you have," comforted Gurri. "There's not a finer watcher in the forest."

"Except on her own behalf," Nello teased.

"D-don't look now, but One-Eye's on your tail," Membo joked.

Perri spun around on her branch. "Up here?" she cried. "Can this fox climb?"

They all laughed silently, and even Perri joined them finally.

"You should be ashamed, making fun of your elders!"

she said. "But as far as watchfulness goes, Geno, you needn't worry. I'll do my best."

Later on, when the sun was almost directly over their heads, Até came to see them.

"Well," he cried gaily, "all asleep except Gurri. Why, you lazybones!" He stretched himself beside the watchful Gurri. "How is it you're awake? What are you thinking of?"

Gurri shifted uneasily.

"Nothing," she said indistinctly.

Até's eyes widened.

"It couldn't possibly be me, now, could it?"

Gurri replied sharply: "Of course not. Why should I think of you?"

"Oh, I don't know," Até grinned. "I think I'm a very good subject for thought."

Geno woke and cut in testily, "You're a good subject for *anxiety*, running around in full daylight when the thunder-stick's about."

"Oh, come now, you gray-coated fuss-budget! Don't you know I believe in fate?"

"Then you are heading for an extremely unpleasant fate, if you ask me!"

Até's reckless eyes gleamed. Larger than any of them, his antlers more mature, he looked extremely handsome as he rested with his head held high.

"My time has not come yet," he declared. "I shall probably die a stiff-legged old buck with fourteen children, and, if I die young, the fault will be yours," he teased Gurri.

"Why will the fault be mine?" Gurri asked with interest.

"Oh, wilier than the serpent!" Até exclaimed. "As though you didn't know that I don't sleep because of you!"

"Shut up and at least let *this* deer sleep, will you?" demanded Membo.

"You croak more hoarsely than the raven," Até said. "You don't know what you're missing, wasting time here when the sun's so warm on the meadow and the pool sparkles like a sweetheart's eyes."

"Listen to the poet!" growled Nello.

Faline chimed in. "I think Geno is right; you really should be more careful, Até."

"Of course he should!" Geno fixed Até with his eyes. "Promise me you'll stop this foolish wandering about by daylight."

"The moon's as beautiful as the sun just now," Gurri murmured.

Até stared at her.

"Perhaps you're right. Perhaps I'll accept your invitation to join you in the moonlight."

"I gave no invitation," replied Gurri coldly.

"I get a message . . . !" chimed in the magpie suddenly from a hazel twig.

"What is it?" demanded Até.

The magpie stared at him with glazed eyes and puffed out, speckled neckband.

"I see a death," she chattered. "I see a fine roe-deer spread helpless on the earth. He is named . . ."

"Spare us the name," Até grinned. "It would be dreadful to meet a neighbor and know him for a ghost already!"

"You're a mocker," the magpie accused him.

"A mocker? Not I! I just face the world as I find it." He looked hard at Gurri. "I'll join you in the moonlight when you do invite me, Gurri. Meantime, I'll stretch my legs."

He got up, his muscles rippling under his shining coat.

"Goodbye, my friends," he said. "Sleep peacefully and dream"–he had not stopped looking at Gurri–"of me."

Gurri felt a curious prickling behind her eyes. Her mother's gaze was on her. Impatient of that understanding glance, Gurri pretended to fall promptly into slumber. Their moment of peace was rudely interrupted. The thunder-stick spoke again, quite close at hand this time. Like an angry wasp they heard the bullet whine its way through the lower leaves.

"Até!" Gurri cried to herself in silent agony. "Até!"

But it was not Até who was struck by the thunder-stick. It was Boso.

Chapter Thirty-Two

SINCE HIS DEFEAT BY GENO, BOSO HAD walked alone among the younger deer. He led the life of a hermit, shunning the paths his fellows took, reversing his mode of living. When they roamed the paths to the tender fields of grass, the salt-lick or the cooling pool, he slept; and when they slept he wandered. His temper was not yet spoiled. He was moody, but he had not yet turned his loneliness to bitterness.

Now that the roe-deer slept by day, he grazed. So

it was that the boy whose training in the hunt had begun under the gamekeeper's teaching, found him in a thicket.

Dressed in a new green shooting suit, the boy carried a light repeating rifle. He still had to bag his first deer.

When he saw Boso, excitement gripped him. True, this deer must be very young because his antlers were so small, but he would have time to worry about that later. The important thing now, at this actual moment, was to get a deer.

The morning light was still clouded with mist, the shot a long and difficult one. Moving down wind, the boy began to stalk his quarry.

Cautiously he moved from bush to bush. Occasionally a twig snapped under his beginner's foot.

Boso started nervously. He had a feeling that danger was near. He began to move, slowly because he was not sure from where the subtle hint of danger came; but soon the quick drumbeat of his hoofs would mean his safety.

The boy flung himself on the ground, his own nerves tense with the fear of disappointment. Hardly sighting in his haste, he brought his rifle up and fired. The bullet, like an evil message, streaked for Boso. Desperately leaping at the rifle's sound, Boso sprang away. He felt his chest sear with a burning pain. With a snort of terror he rushed into the rising sun.

Bambi, on guard, sprang to his feet. Like a flashing shadow his passage through the trees was swift but silent. He met Boso at an angle among the columns of a grove of pine. The young roe-deer was staggering with fear and pain.

"Come," Bambi commanded, "follow me!"

Dumbly Boso obeyed. His blood ran down his chest and made a trail of ruddy spots behind him. He wanted to lie down, to rest, to tremble, alone and quietly, as is the way of wounded deer; but Bambi was firm. He knew the danger of those bloody tracks.

"Hurry," he urged. "We must stop that bleeding or He will surely find you."

They came to a tiny glade where a crystal spring

welled up and fed a lawn of clustering herbs. Bambi chose one.

"Eat that," he said.

Boso took a mouthful of it and spat it out.

"It's horrible," he groaned. "Let me lie down and rest."

"Nonsense," Bambi growled. "You're hardly scratched. I thought you were so brave—such a great fighter! Do you give up when a bramble scratches you?" He grinned suddenly, remembering the time when Boso had burrowed like a rabbit into a tangle of thorns. "Come now, eat, and eat well. That herb will stop your bleeding."

"I've been struck by the thunder-stick," Boso wailed.

"And you're alive to tell about it! You're lucky, my boy. Lucky—and a fool to be out in daylight."

Grudgingly Boso ate the gray-green weed.

"That's it," Bambi said. "That will do."

Bambi made Boso walk in front of him while he keenly eyed the path. When the telltale bloodspots ceased, he halted.

"Now, follow me," he ordered.

Along a twisting course Bambi circled through the

wood. It dawned on Boso that he was returning to his mother's sleeping place. Soon they arrived. Rolla and Lana lay side by side, but Rolla was not asleep.

"Now get in there," Bambi snapped. "Apologize to your mother for causing her so much worry and in the future behave like a deer with brains instead of an empty-headed loon!"

Boso tried to stammer his thanks, but Bambi stopped him short.

"Goodbye," he said. "I have other things to think about."

Bambi could not know that in saving Boso he sacrificed Até. How could he understand the character of this boy in the green shooting suit? Bambi dealt in facts like life and death and love and fear. He did not guess the puny resentment of a pampered youngster, used to getting everything his heart desired.

After losing Boso, the boy came back regularly. Each morning saw him stealing through the forest trees, the magazine of his light rifle loaded not only with shells but with spite. For several days he never saw a deer.

There were skunks and squirrels, but they did not tempt him. His victim was to be a deer or nothing.

Gurri did not invite Até to a moonlight meeting and the young buck kept his threat. He moved boldly about the forest paths, feeling the warm sun on his silken coat, grazing with carefree ease on ripened grass.

Jays and magpies scolded him, but he laughed at them.

"My time is not yet, I tell you," he mocked them. "I shall have fourteen children."

Perri warned him solemnly.

"There is danger in the wood. I have seen Him stalking. Courage is an excellent thing, Até, but rashness deserves the reward it always gets."

"You're worse than the screech-owl with your old sayings," Até cried. "As for me, a long life and a merry one!"

At that moment death grinned at him. The rifle, aimed by spiteful hands, spoke twice.

Até's smile stiffened. His fine muscles, tensing, threw him into the air. Six great leaps to cover he made; and then he died.

Perri heard his last words:

"Gurri, please . . . !"

The gamekeeper came running through the trees just as the jubilant boy broke cover. They met over the still quivering corpse.

"Not two years old!" the gamekeeper ground out. "You young ruffian, didn't I tell you to leave deer under six years old alone?"

The boy grinned cheekily.

"You can leave out the preaching," he sneered. "I'll do what I like around here."

The gamekeeper paused with his hunting knife in his hand.

"You will, eh?" he snapped.

"Yes! And if there are any objections from you, you won't be working long."

The gamekeeper carefully put his knife back in its sheath.

"You're going to go whining to your father, is that it?" he said slowly.

The boy backed away.

"Now listen, you! If you know what's good for you, you'll leave me alone!"

"I will, will I?" Almost absent-mindedly the game-keeper advanced on the young hunter. "Well, I'm not so sure about that."

There was a sharp smacking sound in the forest. The boy's hand flew to his cheek. Tears sprang in his eyes.

"You hit me!" he yelled. "You hit me!"

"Right," said the gamekeeper. "Right you are! Now go along home and tell your father about it, you . . . !"

But he did not finish his sentence. The boy was no longer there.

Chapter Thirty-Three

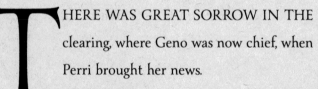

THERE WAS GREAT SORROW IN THE clearing, where Geno was now chief, when Perri brought her news.

"Até," Gurri cried. "Oh no, not Até! I don't believe it."

"I'm afraid it's true," Perri advised her sadly. She was quite out of breath. Torn between her natural desire to spread the news of Até's death and her fear of hurting either Geno or Gurri, she had for long, and unknown to the roe-deer, swung from tree to tree about the clearing like a creature possessed, trying to decide what to do.

Now, with her little forefeet working nervously against her white downy front, she said, "I warned him very seriously, but he wouldn't listen."

"I warned him too," the magpie grumbled. "Dear me, what fools males can be!"

"I warned him very seriously," Perri repeated. "Poor fellow, he was so handsome."

"I should have asked him to walk with me in the moonlight," quavered Gurri. "Oh, Mother!"

Faline comforted her softly.

"How could you know? You cannot blame yourself."

"Not even Bambi could have helped Até—and you know, Bambi helped Boso," Perri interrupted.

"Boso!" Geno exclaimed. "What in the world has happened to Boso?"

"He was wounded, but Bambi saved him. One of my relatives told me about it." And she related the whole story of how Boso escaped from the young Him with Bambi's help.

As though it, too, mourned the passing of the carefree

Até, the weather changed. Clouds obscured the sun. A melancholy rain fell steadily. Once or twice thunder rumbled in the distance, but for the most part rain dripped continually, gathering in murky pools under the trees, running in sluggish rivulets along the forest paths.

The roe-deer stayed in sodden discomfort in their sleeping place, not daring to venture abroad because of the thunder-stick which was heard throughout the forest, whenever the rain did pause briefly to renew its strength.

This threatening sound only served to remind them of Até's death which was, in any case, a constant topic of conversation with them.

Flinching, Gurri would say, almost to herself: "Poor, poor fellow! So gay, so young..."

And Geno would interrupt her: "And Boso, too. Boso was wounded."

"Do you suppose his wound was serious?" Membo asked one night just before the time when they usually went to the meadow.

"Who would know?" demanded Nello. "They say

Boso has turned into a regular hermit, always off by himself."

"How terrible for Rolla and Lana!" Faline exclaimed.

"Why don't we go to see them?" Geno suggested with suppressed excitement.

"How can we?" Nello stirred restlessly. "How do we know we would be welcome?"

They were saved further argument by the unexpected appearance of Rolla herself.

"Rolla!" Faline exclaimed.

"I just *couldn't* stay away a moment longer!" Rolla burst out. "What with Boso being well and everything, I just *had* to come. Please don't be angry with me any more. I believe I shall die if you are."

Faline felt her heart soften.

"Rolla," she cried, "I'm really glad to see you. It's been terrible having no one to talk to. Where are the children?"

"Boso," Rolla called, "come here at once!"

Timidly Boso came forward. All of them noticed the scar across his chest. Gurri ran to meet him.

"Please join us, Boso."

Boso was obviously ill at ease. Rolla said quickly:

"Bambi saved him! Isn't it wonderful? He wants to thank him, to say he's sorry to you and Geno, don't you, Boso?"

"Why, Rolla," Faline interrupted, "we owe you at least as deep an apology as you do us. As for what Bambi did I'm sure it's enough reward to see Boso alive and well and to have you all with us."

"But where is Lana?" Geno cried.

"I'm here," she answered shyly, joining them.

"Am I forgiven?" Geno whispered.

"Of course. I was stupid."

"Well," said Nello, "this is more sweetness and light than I've seen in a long time!" Then he asked, "You said Bambi saved you?"

Boso threw his head up. "He certainly did! I think Bambi's the greatest Prince who ever lived in the forest."

"All but one," said a sepulchral voice.

They looked up and saw the screech-owl.

"W-who was ever g-greater than Bambi?" stuttered Membo wrathfully.

"I don't know his name," the screech-owl replied, "but his fame lives on."

"What did he do?" asked Geno.

"He attacked and overthrew Him."

"I don't believe it," Geno declared stoutly. "When Bambi rescued Gurri from His den, he did the greatest thing that was ever done."

"There was a Prince who attacked Him in single combat and got the better of Him."

"It isn't true, is it, Mother?" As though he was a fawn again, Geno found himself appealing to Faline.

"There is a story that runs something like that," Faline admitted slowly, "but no one knows if it is true or just a myth coming from wishful thinking."

"Wishful thinking?" repeated Lana doubtfully.

Faline was enjoying this sudden return of her authority.

"Yes," she explained, "wishful thinking is to believe something is the truth because you wish to believe it."

"That makes sense," Nello declared shortly, "more sense than the screech-owl's just saying it's true without proof."

"Where there's smoke there's fire," the screech-
owl remarked. He scraped his claws on the branch
on which he was perched and blew his feathers out
grandly. "There are more things in heaven and earth
than are dreamt of in your philosophy."

He managed to make his voice sound very boom-
ing, and there was silence for a moment.

"I think that's right," he concluded anxiously.

"It doesn't make any sense to me," Boso grumbled.
"Listen," he turned to Geno, "why don't we all go to the
meadow to play? I haven't had a good game almost
since I can remember."

"It's getting late, too," Nello put in.

Jostling and chattering, they made their way to the
meadow. The screech-owl flew above them, keeping his
wide eyes open for danger.

"It's wonderful, being together again," whispered
Lana to Gurri as they drew up at the rear of the troop.

"Do you like Membo and Nello?"

"Oh yes, they're sweet."

Rolla, just ahead of them, turned to Faline.

"Too bad Membo stutters," she said.

Faline answered sharply, "We don't mind it. We really love him the more for it."

Rolla bridled. "Oh, but really, Faline, you misunderstand me. . . ."

Lana remarked thoughtfully. "I was jealous of them once, Gurri."

"Why?"

"Because they replaced us. *We* never went with anyone else after you."

"Mother invited them into the family, and I'm glad she did. They've been so good for Geno."

"Yes," Lana agreed with conviction, "they are nice."

"Mother," Gurri called, "I've a feeling Father is around somewhere."

"I'm almost afraid to meet him," declared Boso.

"Y-you needn't be," Membo reassured him. "B-bambi's kind. He understands everything."

"He looks as though he could see right through you."

"I believe he does know more or less what we're thinking."

Conversation died when they reached the meadow. Until the first glimmer of dawn, they ran and played, enjoying their companionship to the full. Only Faline was upset. Once when Gurri passed her, she said:

"Gurri, I feel, as you did, that your father is here."

Faline and Gurri were right in their feeling. Ever since the young He had slain Até, Bambi had kept close watch on His comings and goings. Whenever He came to the forest, Bambi awaited Him and, close behind Him, trailed His every step.

Perhaps Bambi did not realize how great a need there was for caution. The boy returned to the forest, seeking only vengeance.

He had gone to his father to report the gamekeeper's assault upon him. He had painted the simple story in lurid detail. His father had rebuffed him.

Even now the boy could not believe it. This father, generally so indulgent, had almost balanced the gamekeeper's blow with one on the other cheek.

Brooding over this situation, the boy decided on a means of revenge. He would pay his debt to the gamekeeper by shooting more deer, any deer—even if they were week-old fawns.

Several times the young He was successfully out-witted by Bambi. Sometimes he would send a magpie with an urgent message for some unsuspecting buck picking his carefree way to the pool, or command Perri to race and warn some wanderer near the salt-lick.

Failing to get a close shot, the boy discarded his own light rifle and stole a special gun of his father's: a weapon of small caliber but terrific power. Armed with this, he prowled the forest from the first crack of dawn until the gloom of night was thickening above the trees.

Even without Bambi's interference, the task he had set himself was difficult, for it rained incessantly and the deer kept to cover.

Quite by accident he stumbled on the meadow where Faline, Rolla and the children played. Dawn had not yet broken, and the weather was clear. The sight of eight roe-deer frolicking with such lack of caution surpassed his highest hopes.

It was a fine herd.

He crept stealthily to the edge of the forest and watched them.

Behind him came Bambi.

The magpies and the squirrels were fast asleep. The owl, Bambi's only hope, cried mournfully but far away. There was no one he could send as messenger. He was troubled. He must act—and act fast.

The young He was between him and the field. To dash past Him was to invite certain death, not only for himself, but also for some members of his family. For Bambi knew that the thunder-stick spoke more than once and that quickly.

If he circled the clearing and entered from the other side, the same danger existed. He would have to leave cover and, worse than that, the young He would be unobserved for a period of minutes.

During those minutes anything could happen.

The youth rose to his knees and reached into a leather case he wore slung about his shoulders to extract a pair of night glasses. Through them he examined the herd again. There were two magnificent roes, but no full-grown buck was with them. Filled with disappointment, he rested his glasses on Geno—young, but well built and with small, new antlers.

Geno would do.

Silently the boy steadied himself on one knee, dropped his glasses, lifted his rifle and cuddled it against his cheek.

At that moment, Bambi, too, acted.

Lowering his mighty antlers he shot from his hiding place.

Like a stone from a sling he charged the boy, his antlers driving straight at the boy's back.

An unheard-of sound of human fear and anguish rose high among the trees. The thunder-stick went off, but the bullet discharged straight upward.

Bambi leaped over his adversary and disappeared into the shadows. The roe-deer in the meadow had already fled. The screech-owl came hurrying through the trees like a thing possessed, almost flattening his face, which was already flat enough, against the trunks of trees.

He cried as he flew:

"The hero's name is Bambi! Bambi attacked Him!"

The whole forest was awake. From the smallest wren to the hovering crows, from the tiniest mouse to One-Eye himself, the news spread in a flood of joyous chatter.

Only the Kings remained aloof.

Perhaps, in their majesty, they never heard of this great feat; perhaps they disdained to gossip of it; perhaps they were jealous that it was not one of their own great tribe whose fame rang far and wide.

Wearily, spent with excitement, the screech-owl perched upon a branch. Over and over he muttered to himself:

"After me, the deluge!"

The robin, anxious to create his bit of history, flew to the spot where the young He had been. No boy was there now, but the thunder-stick lay among the bushes where it had been dropped.

The robin flew down and perched upon it.

Chapter Thirty-Four

O LONGER WAS THE FOREST disturbed by the report of the thunder-stick. The boy, abashed by the way the tables had been turned on him, took to his bed.

Full of excitement, young birds adventured from their nests, fluttering with breathless squeaks from twig to twig. One-Eye, trotting along a forest path, watched them with a contemplative eye. He was not hungry and creatures so weak did not make good sport; yet he felt that, perhaps, one snap at them would give him satisfaction.

He stopped abruptly when he saw the shadow in the underbrush.

"Bambi?" he asked.

It was a long time since Bambi had been seen in the forest. Following his adventure with the young Him, he had vanished from sight. Many had sought him, but none had been able to track him down.

"Quite a stranger!" One-Eye said, grinning.

"That's how I prefer to be with you," Bambi remarked.

"Of course!" One-Eye spoke in his oiliest tones. "You're very famous, now. The whole forest speaks of you as though you were already a legend. I should be honored that you speak to me at all."

"If it's an honor," Bambi told him, "it's very unwillingly bestowed. What I did, I did because I had to."

"It was heroic of you," said One-Eye with sly flattery.

Bambi shook his head. "Is it heroic to do what necessity demands?" He wheeled and disappeared.

One-Eye went on his way thoughtfully. His mouth felt dry and he headed for the pool. Evening was advancing quickly and the birds were silent.

Faline was still lying in the clearing, but she was alone. It seemed to her that this had become almost a normal condition. Geno, Gurri, Nello and Membo had affairs to attend to that took them from her side. She sighed, realizing that as the little birds were now learning to fly, so too her children would be leaving her.

She was thinking of the time of separation that must come to all the people of the forest, when she heard the slightest rustle in the thicket by the oak tree. Perri flirted her tail as she quickly turned to spy out the intruder.

"It's Bambi," she said. "Greetings, Bambi."

"Greetings, Perri." Bambi came out into the center of the clearing. "So you are alone, Faline."

Faline rose. "Yes," she said simply. "I am alone often now."

"Yes." Bambi's voice was grave. "The time has come."

Faline's voice quivered. "It is a little hard to see them go."

"I know. Will you be strong and tell them?"

"I . . ." She hesitated. "Must it be at once?"

"I'm afraid so. Would you rather they told you?" His tone became suddenly gay. "Do you remember how independent we were in our youth?"

"Oh, Bambi," she cried, "it's not a joking matter!"

"I know. So you must tell them, in the words only a mother can find."

"And you—will you be leaving me too?"

He nuzzled her affectionately. "You know better than that, Faline. After you, I have my duties. The children must be taught the lore of the forest, the secrets of woodcraft. But very soon I shall come back. You know that, Faline."

She knew it. She watched him go with new comfort in her heart.

Beside the pool, Geno, Lana, Boso and Gurri stood in restrained silence.

"The earth looks altogether different tonight," sighed Lana. "The moon is as bright as hope, the breeze is soft."

"The grass is so green and smooth I hardly like to eat it," Geno said.

Boso whispered to Gurri: "I'll never be as handsome as Até, I know, but I could try to take his place. . . ."

"You're very modest tonight," Gurri replied softly.

Geno lifted his head high and sniffed the air.

"Lana's right. There is a difference. I feel bigger, as though I were a part of everything and everything was locked in me. Father was right. We are one with the trees and they with us. We have the same need to grow and flourish and sink our own roots into the earth; and so long as there is earth, both they and we will go on side by side."

He stopped when he saw his sister shiver.

"What is it?" he asked.

The screech-owl, lighting on his apple branch, answered him.

"It's that fox again," he said.

Geno was able to make out the shadow moving at the forest's edge.

"So it is," he said contemptuously. "But don't be afraid of him, Gurri. He won't hurt you."

"I can't help it." Gurri shuddered.

One-Eye left the shadows to cross the meadow. Geno met him, head lowered, Boso not far behind.

"Well," said One-Eye, "if you don't get more like your father every day!"

"What do you want?"

"A drink. Nothing more, I assure you."

Geno moved slowly aside.

"Well, all right, go and get it. But don't imagine you can catch us as you tried to catch the heron."

"The heron!" One-Eyed murmured, remembering. "Of course, you were there, weren't you?" His single eye gleamed evilly.

Gurri and Lana cried almost in one breath: "Be careful, Geno!"

Geno disregarded them. He snorted disdainfully.

"Of course I was there and it was then that I learned how to handle you."

One-Eye managed a grin.

"I really should lose my temper with you, but in view of the respect in which I hold your father . . ." he licked the end of his nose reflectively . . . "I'll just bid you goodbye."

The screech-owl chuckled.

"Well, I always did say that time changes everything. . . . Yet, on the other hand . . ."

Geno grinned himself.

"Don't contradict that one," he said. "That's the truth."

Gurri gave a last shudder as she heard the sound of One-Eye lapping at the pool.

"If only I could get over being frightened of those creatures . . . !" She sighed. "You're very brave, Geno."

Geno seemed hardly to notice the compliment.

"Let's go home," he said. "Mother is alone."

He led them trotting back toward the clearing. In the pathway the hare sat upright, a silver statuette of fur and moonlight.

"Greetings, friend hare," Gurri called.

"Oh, greetings!" The hare jerked nervously to face them as they came. "That fox, now. Have you seen him?"

"He's safe enough down by the pool. Geno took care of him," Boso cried.

"Geno!" The hare sat upright as an exclamation point. "Oh, cunning and treachery—Geno!"

He watched them running by. Two crows looked down at them sleepily, their crops were full, their plumage shone. A robin dreamed of the thunder-stick. He dragged it from the ground like a long worm and swallowed it. A magpie stirred.

"I get a message . . . !" she cried in a faint echo of her waking voice.

Faline awaited them in the clearing. The moon was sinking low. It gleamed on the mighty, motionless branches of the oak. It outlined the sapling, stronger now, grown a little now, with poison ivy not so high upon its shoulders. The great pine stood up black and proud, never sleeping, hardly ever rustling. The maple leaves whispered with the passage of some night prowler bent on getting home before the dawn arrived. The owl's far, melancholy voice was heard.

"Hah-ah, hah-aha!"

"It's nice to see you children all together," Faline said. "It's been a long time. . . ."

"Oh, Mother," Gurri cried, "we've been thoughtless."

Faline smiled at them lovingly. "Not thoughtless at all. You can't be tied to me forever."

Slowly Membo and Nello came through the trees. Faline embraced them with a look.

"All of you," she said. "All of you together. What a family!"

Impulsively Gurri said, "We'll never leave you alone again."

Faline smiled again. "Oh yes, you will. How can I continue to look after such great, hulking children? You are grown up. Why, just look at Geno's crown . . . !"

She stopped. Geno said soberly:

"You're sending us away!"

The silence that grew between them was the silence of understanding.

"That's right," Faline told them gently. She had it now, all the courage that the forest and the life within it gave to her. "That's right, my dear. I'm sending you away."

"N-no!" stammered Membo wretchedly.

"Yes, my son. You and your brother have both grown strong and quick. My task is finished. You, Gurri, will go—and Geno, too."

Geno said softly, "You are good to us, Mother."

For a moment Faline gazed at him steadily. "You understand, don't you, my son?" she said; and then, to their surprise, she left them abruptly.

Boso said, "We must go home. We, too, must be free." He turned to Membo. "You and your brother must join with me. That is, if Geno . . ."

Geno shook his head. "No," he said. "I think . . ."

He looked up quickly. A shadow moved where the morning mist hung thickest.

"Father," he cried, "will you teach me the lore of the forest, how to be a shadow moving in it as you do . . . ?"

"Find your sleeping place, my son, and when night falls we'll begin."

Faline stood alone, not so far from the thicket that she could not hear what passed there. She knew them as they went, each one of them: Geno's eager hooves, the

lighter steps of Gurri, the brothers slowly stepping in time like a single animal.

A quiet shape with its long legs tucked behind drifted high above her—the heron going in the morning to his stream. She heard an agitated twittering in the trees above her. Two finches were flying wearily from branch to branch.

"What is it?" she asked gently.

"It's our son, our great big son. . . ." replied the mother bird.

"Who ate more at a sitting than a regiment of crows in a week," quavered her mate.

"He's gone away from us. . . ."

"Without a word . . . except to grumble at the size of the nest and the worms I brought. . . . My goodness, they were as big as garter snakes. I almost broke my neck dragging them out of the ground."

"You're always grumbling, finch," his mate accused him.

"I'm sorry, my love."

"And so you should be!" Her voice broke. "Such a son he was. We had such plans for him. . . ."

"Well, he's gone," sighed the father.

A cuckoo, Faline thought. She felt happy suddenly. All the children of the forest came to the time of leaving, only some of them were good children and some were bad.

Hers were gone, but they would come again and they were good children.

"They go," she murmured to the finches, "and the better they are, the more we miss them. But they must go. That is the fate of all parents."

She saw a well-beloved shadow move with usual silence just where the tree trunks stood in mist.

With light and quickened step she went toward it.